FOREVER, MY CHARLIE

Dayne Winters

To Judy, with love
When I posed the idea of writing a novel, you were as
excited as I was. When I was writing it, you helped me
think of just the right word, which sentence was better,
and made us delicious dinners. When it was time to revise
and edit the book, you helped me make the corrections.
When it was time to publish, we worked together figuring
out how to do it. When the book came out, you gave
me all the credit. This book is for you, Judy. XXOO

CONTENTS

ACKNOWLEDGEMENTS

Thank you so much to the intrepid Beta readers who generously gave of their time and expertise to improve the manuscript. This book is so much better because of their ideas and sharp eyes. Thank you Liz, Nancy, Judy, Melanie, Barbara and Mardale. You guys are the best! Remaining errors are all on me.

January 1985 - August 1992

My father left my mom in 1985, when I was just two months old. While I grew up without a father, my mom, my grandma, and my Aunt Rose; three strong, independent, exasperating, women worked together to raise me and ensured that I knew I was loved.

My mom worked the day shift at the nearby Target in our hometown of Mountain View, Idaho. While mom was at work, my grandma took care of me. Her house was just a half mile down the road from our house which made it easy to drop me off early in the morning and pick me back up in the late afternoon when she got off work.

Grandma lived in an old farmhouse that she and Grandad had lovingly restored. From what I could tell from the pictures Grandma showed me, it looked like the farmhouse had needed a lot of work when they bought it. And apparently, I was right, since to this day my mom, and Aunt Rose, frequently complain that when their friends were off having fun on weekends and school breaks, the sisters were hard at work as unpaid laborers fixing-up that old house. Still, it made them handy with tools.

Grandma was 5'2" tall and a little rounder than she would have liked, but I loved everything about her. She was soft and warm, and she smelled like angel food cake. No one hugged better than she did. Before I loved to cuddle with her on the couch as we watched her favorite soap opera '*The Edge of Night*' together.

My mom looked nothing like Grandma. She'd taken after her father. Mom was a willowy 5'8" but her hugs were almost as good as Grandma's and her laugh made me laugh. Her brown eyes twinkled when she smiled, and she always sang in the kitchen.

Grandma's hair was almost completely gray, but mom had beautiful, dark brown hair, thanks to Lady Clairol. I wasn't allowed to ask Aunt Rose about her hair color.

Aunt Rose was a big woman, tall like Mom, but padded like Grandma. I loved spending time with her. She had a big laugh that demanded you laugh right along with her. She was always up for an adventure and treated me more like a younger sister and co-conspirator than as a responsibility. We loved to dream up pranks to play on Grandma or Mom. She didn't have much of a filter. What she thought just came right out of her mouth. After a glass of wine, there was no telling what she might say.

Neither Mom nor Grandma talked about my father. *Ever.* Aunt Rose was my only source of information. From my aunt I gleaned little bits about him, here and there, over the years. So, what little I knew about my father was courtesy of her.

One day when we were looking through one of Aunt Rose's old photo albums, we came to some wedding pictures of my parents. I had never seen these before which was strange since my mom and I often looked through her photo albums together. In the pictures, mom, and my father both looked so happy. Mom was beautiful in a white, lacey dress that went all the way to the floor, and my father wearing a suit, looked so proud standing tall and stiff beside her.

My aunt studied the picture. "Your father was such a handsome guy," she sighed. "He was a lot of fun, too. All the girls in town were jealous of your mom. When he walked out on you and her, it shocked everyone, but especially your mom."

Curious, I worked up my courage to ask a question I had always wondered about. "Why did he leave us, Aunt Rose? Was he mad at Mom...*or me*?" I asked in a small voice

Realizing that she probably shouldn't have said the part about my dad leaving, my aunt leaned in close and kissed me on the forehead. She tried to reassure me that nothing about my father leaving was my fault. "Your dad loved you, Pumpkin. I'm sure he never *wanted* to leave, but in some ways, he just wasn't ready for the responsibilities of fatherhood. The changes that come along with a new baby can be a difficult time for some men who for the first time having to share their kingdom. The disruption, the work, the noise, and the responsibility of a new baby were just too much for him. Let's just say he was an idiot and let's leave it at that." So, I did. But I still wondered.

I didn't really understand all of what she'd said, but the words stuck with me. My father had loved my mother. But everything changed when I was born, and I caused disruption, extra work, and noise. I didn't know what a kingdom was, but I now knew that I had wrecked his.

It made me sad. And it made me worry. If I talked too much, or made too much noise, or made a mess, or made too much extra work for Mom or Grandma or Aunt Rose leave, could they leave too? I decided to be more careful. After that I also quit asking about my father, but I still sometimes wondered if he might come back some day. I thought that maybe I could do better if I had a second chance.

When I was five, I started kindergarten and my mother resurrected her pre-marriage ambition to go to nursing school. She applied and was admitted to the Nursing Program at Boise State University's Mountain View satellite campus. To help with expenses, she applied for every grant and scholarship she could find. I can still see her so clearly, working on filling out application after application for grants and scholarships at that old desk. In the end, she was awarded three scholarships and two grants. Together with her job at Target, this would provide enough money to keep us going while she finished up her degree.

We turned one of the bedrooms into a study for her. We had so much fun going to thrift stores to furnish it. We found a dusty, old wooden teacher's desk that would clean up nicely, a leather office chair that swiveled and was in great condition and splurged on an almost new computer that we didn't know how to use.

Of course, things were different after Mom started school. I missed the way it had been when she and I were the center of one another's lives. I missed spending time with her. I didn't have many friends. I mostly had my family. With Mom so busy now, I was lonely. I once asked her if I could have a dog so I wouldn't feel so lonesome. Her face dropped and I thought she was going to cry. After that, she made sure we spent every Sunday together. Just the two of us. I didn't ask about a dog again but sometimes I still felt lonely.

Most of her classes were during the day, so Mom changed her shift at the warehouse from days to nights. I did all I could to help by drying the dishes, keeping my room clean and staying quiet while she studied.

In the summer before second grade Aunt Rose told me about her, now ex-boyfriend. She'd just discovered he was two-timing her. "Come to think of it, most of the men I've dated have turned out to be jerks. As often happened when talking with adults about important things, I wasn't sure what "two timing" meant. Something to do with math, maybe? Aunt Rose took a long breath and continued. Maybe it's just the way of the world," she continued resignedly. "Look at your dad. He left your mother with nothing and never paid a cent of child support. Your mom has had a hard time of it."

I wasn't sure exactly what child support was, but by the expression on Aunt Rose's face I knew not paying it must be bad —and once again I saw it was my fault. That night I asked Mom what "two-timing" was, and she confirmed it was multiplying by two, something I would learn in the third grade.

Still, I was grateful to my aunt for these small glimpses into my past and insights into my parents' history. Based on Mom and Grandma's silence and Aunt Rose's tone of voice, I figured if my father ever did come back, they would all give him a tongue-lashing to remember. Having myself reaped the consequences of disappointing any one of them, I might have to feel a little sorry for him for disappointing all three

As I got older, I tried to find more ways to help Mom around the house. I remembered that one of the reasons my father had left us was that I made too much work for him. I added vacuuming, dusting, and taking out the garbage to my list of responsibilities. It made me feel safer and I was able to lighten mom's workload.

Even while so much was changing with Mom going to school and working nights, there were many routines that stayed the same even with Mom's work and school. One of these was our special "First Day of School Breakfast" which consisted of waffles shaped like an old-fashioned schoolhouse drizzled with butter and the raspberry syrup that my grandma canned each summer. After my favorite breakfast in the world, we cleaned up together, I grabbed my new backpack, and we were off to school. Mom would always drive me to school on the first day. This year I would be entering the second grade.

CHAPTER 1

September 8, 1992 - April 1994

Mom slid her two-toned 1978 Chevy Impala into the student drop-off area. Mom loved that car. It had been her dad's. He gave it to her as a wedding present in1982, the year before he died. Grandma said Mom treated that old Impala like the sister I never had, and I agree with her.

Shifting the cherry and tan muscle car into park, Mom leaned across the soft leather seat to kiss me on the forehead for luck and wished me "a brilliant start to my first day of second grade."

"I love you, Jory. I'll be waiting to hear all about your first day when you get home."

"I love you too, Mom." I responded breezily, excited to start the day.

I pushed hard to open the heavy car door and jumped out. I made sure that I stayed within the crosswalk that had been painted onto the deep black asphalt. I turned back for a quick, reassuring wave from my mother as she pulled away from the curb. Another mother immediately eased her car forward to drop off her kids. The crossing guard, Ms. Morales, watched to make sure I made it to the sidewalk. I remembered her from last year. She was nice.

An open gate in the chain-link fence led into the playground. I went to Mountain View Elementary in kindergarten and first grade and so, knew my way around. I saw that some kids were playing four-square, tetherball, and tag. Others stood around in groups just talking. Spotting a group of mostly second graders, I made my way toward them. As I got closer, I noticed a girl I didn't recognize. She was tall and dark and had the most beautiful long brown hair, strands of which glittered red and gold in the morning sun. She looked happy and excited to be here, not quiet and shy like me. For a moment our eyes met, and her smile made me want to smile back at her. Before I could join the group, the morning bell abruptly signaled the start of the 1992-93 school year.

Along with the other second-graders, I hurried to the blue door that led into Mrs. Grove's second grade classroom. I noticed the new girl was coming too. Mrs. Grove was waiting just inside the door. She welcomed each of us to her class and pointed out a table at the back of the room where we should pick up our name-tag and desk assignment.

I took a few moments to look around my classroom for the next year. The desks had been aligned in neat rows facing Mrs. Grove's desk just in front of the chalkboard. I envied the teacher's chair which looked much more comfortable than our desk seats. The dark green surface of the chalkboard was gleaming in the sunlight that poured in through the windows. Everything looked shiny and new. The room still smelled of new paint.

I found my nametag and saw that I had been assigned a seat at one of the tandem student desks. Mine was in the third row. I sat down at my new desk and turned to see what I could see. There were many colorful posters on the walls: planets and plants and the ocean and bugs and a pretty one about being kind to others. I noticed two doors at the back of the room. One looked like a storage closet and the other was our own small restroom! This could be a good year, I hoped to myself.

Mrs. Grove announced that those of us who had found their desks should begin putting their supplies into them. I wiggled a little in anticipation. My favorite thing about every school year was getting a new backpack and fresh school supplies. I loved it when all the supplies were still in their packages and just waiting to be used in the first assignments of the year. I liked the smell of them and the crisp edges of everything. The second-best part was taking each item out, one-at-a-time and placing it carefully into my new desk. I frowned a little as I thought about my least favorite thing, which was the first time I made a hole in my paper trying to erase a mistake. But I would not worry about that right now. I liked that my desk was so clean, a fitting home to my fresh supplies. I rechecked every item as I stowed it away:

Big Chief wide-lined tablet
Package of six #2 yellow pencils
Pink Pearl eraser
Ruler, inches on one side, millimeters on the other
Package of 24 Crayola brand crayons
Small pair of scissors with rounded tips

I just loved the first day of school! I glanced around to see what everyone else was doing and saw the new girl walking toward me. Like me, was wearing shorts and a blouse. Her shorts were dark blue and mine were tan. Her blouse was white and sleeveless; mine was short-sleeved and a peachy color that I really loved. But we were both wearing navy blue flip-flops! Something about our similar outfits and matching flip-flops seemed to connect us, and I felt happy. I was hoping her desk would be near mine.

She came to a stop at my desk and carefully compared the number of her desk assignment to the number on the tandem desk where I sat. Now certain that she was in the right place, she sat down at the other half of my desk, turned in her seat to see me better and smiled at me. I wanted to say something, but the words got stuck in my throat. Pretty usual for me. She looked around at the posters for a second, just as I had. I watched her take her things out of her backpack and begin shoving them into her desk with no concern for how things would fit best and be easiest to find. I frowned as I considered her lack of organization and apparent comfort with it.

When she had finished emptying her backpack, she looked at me for a second like she knew I'd been watching her and said, "My name is Charlotte Young, but you can call me Charlie. We just moved to Mountain View two weeks ago. This is my first day at this school."

"My name is Jory Santos. I've gone here since kindergarten." I wanted to say more, but I didn't have a nickname and couldn't think of anything else to tell her. Conversation had never come easily to me. I felt frustrated for always being "the quiet girl."

After a moment or two Charlie asked, "Would you like to be my friend?"

I shyly looked up at her and smiled. All I could get out was, "Mm-hmm!" But what I thought was, Charlie wants to be friends with me! I could hardly believe it!

Charlie smiled at me as she asked, "Do you want to play with me at recess?"

"Yes!" I thought. But tongue tied, I could only nod.

Charlie's face split into an enormous grin that brightened the entire room. Her warm hazel eyes seemed to dance as she put her hand in mine. "This is going to be the best year ever!" she said. And it was. I just knew that Charlie was going to be my very first *best* friend!

That day was the first of many that I would thank the universe for bringing Charlie into my life. We were best friends from then on. Who could resist such a smile?

Charlie wasn't exaggerating when she said that she and her family had just arrived in Mountain View. Charlie's parents, Adele and Jack Young, had moved into the rustic Clear Springs Lake Resort only two weeks before school started. They had purchased the resort and were going to live on site and run it themselves. It was on 150 acres about six miles outside of Mountain View. The resort featured a 90-acre spring-fed private lake, 16 cabins, an eight-room lodge with a separate owners' suite and attached mother-in-law apartment, a fishing tackle shop, a recreational equipment rental shack and two boat docks. It needed work, but the Youngs thought it had the potential to become a great vacation destination. Charlie's parents had been busy every day since their arrival.

The lodge was beautiful with its exposed timbers of red oak, and hardwood floors throughout. Large windows looked out on the forest and lake. Oversized upholstered chairs and couches took advantage of the views outside and the large stone fireplace that was the centerpiece of the inside of the lodge. Its twelve guest rooms were clean and comfortable.

The cedar shake cabins ranged from one to three bedrooms. They were simple but comfortable. Each cabin sported a wrap-around porch, eat-in kitchen, and large living area with a wood-burning fireplace. They furniture matched those in the lodge, but on a smaller scale. Colorful Adirondack chairs welcomed guests to the cabins. In the spring and summer, the lodge and cabins were most always fully booked. Fishing, canoeing, kayaking, hiking, and biking kept guests engaged and entertained. In the winter it was less busy, but guests still visited the resort for snowshoeing, cross-country skiing, snowmobiling, or just to enjoy a cozy fire and breathtaking scenery.

At school Charlie and I were inseparable, but we saw little of one another after school or on weekends. Charlie's chores at the Clear Springs Lake Resort often kept her busy afternoons and weekends. Even when she didn't have chores to do, the resort was four miles from my house which, our parents thought it was too far to walk or bike ride on our own. This meant we didn't see one another outside of school unless our parents were willing to drive us.

Charlie's parents were always busy running the lodge and Mom was always busy working and studying to be a nurse. We looked forward to the time we could ride our bikes back and forth without having to rely on our parents for transportation. But we talked on the phone almost every day. I still couldn't believe that Charlie had picked me to be her best friend!

CHAPTER 2

May 7, 1994

May 7th was a big day in the Santos household. Mom was graduating from Boise State University with a Bachelor of Science in Nursing! It took her five years of perseverance and plain willpower to earn her bachelor's degree, taking courses during the day, working full time at night and raising me. All of us were so proud of her. The university auditorium was filled with more people than I had ever seen in one place before. Mom looked radiant in her blue cap and gown adorned with yellow braided rope showing that she was graduating with honors. The Dean of the College of Nursing called, "Tess Santos," and my mom walked across the stage to receive her diploma, with joyful tears in her eyes. Everyone clapped as loud as we could. Grandma, Aunt Rose, and I all had tears in our eyes, too. We knew how hard Mom had worked for this: a full-time job, a full-time student, and a full-time mother. She had also distinguished herself with honors! She'd really made it!

We went to a special dinner at Stuart Anderson's Black Angus Restaurant to celebrate. I'd never been in such a fancy restaurant before. Aunt Rose was treating everyone and said I could order whatever I wanted. It took me a long time to figure out what "whatever" was going to be, but that was okay because Grandma, Mom and Aunt Rose seemed never run out of things to talk about. I poured over the menu while they chatted. I finally chose the Petite Sirloin Steak Dinner that came with a green salad and baked potato with four different toppings! The one that was called "chives" looked like green onion tops to me, but it was delicious on my potato. I made a mental note to try this at home.

After I ordered, Aunt Rose whispered to me that "petite" is pronounced "*puh*-**teet**" and not "**pee**-*tit*" as I had pronounced it. At first, I felt embarrassed that I had said the word wrong, but one look at Mom and Grandma's faces and we all just laughed and laughed together.

Mom and Grandma had wine with dinner. I had a Coke. Aunt Rose was drinking only club soda because she was the designated driver. We toasted Mom many times. I'd never seen my family so happy.

Mom's license arrived about six weeks after she sat for the licensure exam, but she had already begun applying for jobs and even had an interview scheduled with Three Rivers Hospital in town. Notice of her passing score from the Licensing Board came in the mail just three days before her interview. They offered her a rotating shift position on the orthopedic unit which she accepted straight away.

CHAPTER 3

Summer 1996 - Summer 1999

At the beginning of summer vacation between the 4th and 5th grade, Charlie's and my mom decided we were old enough to ride our bikes back and forth to one another's house. We promised to be extra careful, only ride during daylight hours, follow all the safety rules, *and* call our moms both before we left *and* when we arrived, so neither would worry. Even then, we didn't get to spend as much time together as we would have liked.

There was always something that needed to be done at the lodge, cabins, or lake. As the oldest of three kids, Charlie had the most chores and couldn't play until her chores were done. We overcame that obstacle by asking Charlie's mom if I could help Charlie with her chores. After that I often biked over on weekend mornings to help Charlie finish her work more quickly. That gave us time to take a kayak or canoe out onto the lake and float the afternoon away. Sometimes we'd take a hike along the trails that ran across the property and into the state forest that surrounded the resort on three sides.

One Sunday, after helping Charlie clean the equipment and the cabins, Mrs. Young asked me if I'd like to earn a little extra money as an official employee of the resort. "Just on weekends," Mrs. Young explained, "I figure you might as well get paid for work you're already doing. And don't think I haven't noticed that you get more done than Charlie!"

"No way is Jory faster than I am!" Charlie protested, her competitive streak rising.

"Way." Mrs. Young confirmed. "I've followed behind both of you to check your work. When you work as a team you get more than twice as much done as you do on your own and the quality is always better."

She turned to me, "I'd need you for four hours every Saturday from 11:00 to 3:00 unless we agree to something different in advance. I can pay you each $5.00 an hour." Nodding towards Charlie, she said, "We have an arrangement with Charlie. Half of everything she earns goes into her college fund. She gets to keep the other half for spending money. But you, Jory, would get the full $5.00 per hour. If your mom wants you to put some of your wages into savings, you and your mom can work that out."

She continued, "If you finish all your assigned cabins before your four hours are up, you can use whatever time you have left to clean up life jackets, canoes and kayaks."

Mrs. Young directed her gaze to me. "I've already talked with your mother about this, and she thinks it's a fine idea so long as it's only on Saturdays and your grades don't suffer." She smiled at me, "So, what do you think, Jory?"

"It sounds great! When do I start?" $20.00 for 4 hours of work seemed like a ton of money to me! My mind flashed on the 5-speed mountain bike that I had been dreaming of for the last 6 months. I knew there was no way I could ask my mom to buy it for me. Now, in just five weeks I could afford it myself! I had to force myself not to jump up and down, and I could see Charlie's excitement too.

When Charlie and I turned 12, Mrs. Young increased our pay by 25 cents an hour and increased our hours a little here and there. There was still plenty of time for Charlie and me to enjoy the resort after we finished our work. I had a few other friends but none as close as Charlie. We remained inseparable into Junior High.

In the 1997-98 school year, Charlie and I were in the 7th grade. Although our friendship was still strong, other things began to change. We were growing up, maturing, and developing. We watched as girls in our class began to go "boy crazy." We saw the drama and stress it caused and the friendships it damaged. We made a pact to never let a boy come between us. When we mentioned this to Mrs. Young, she said that we would never have to worry because we were always so busy doing things together, we didn't have any time to go "boy crazy."

She called us the "troublesome twosome." We earned that title through a couple of itty-bitty mistakes we made at work. Once, when we were a little too enthusiastically shaking out the bedding from one of the cabins, we broke both lamps on the nightstands next to the bed. We were scared nearly to death to have to tell Mrs. Young, though we laughed about it later. We had to pay for the broken lamps out of our paychecks.

The second episode was more embarrassing, but less expensive. We were listening to music as we were cleaning a cabin and I was pretending the vacuum cleaner was my dance partner. As I was coming to the final dip move at the end of the song, my feet got caught up in the cord. I lost my balance, causing my dance partner and me to plunge to the ground, resulting in a mildly sprained ankle and highly bruised ego. I limped for a week.

We never told Mrs. Young about the time we misread the cabin number she assigned us to clean and surprised the guests just as they were coming out of the shower. We were so embarrassed; we turned and ran out of the cabin as fast as we could! Thank goodness the guests were good sports about it. Looking back on it, the little trouble we got into was pretty tame stuff.

About that time, I started to notice something that disturbed me. Mr. Young seemed to have taken a sudden and unexplained dislike to me. Surely, he hadn't always been as gruff and stern toward me as he was now? It was a distinct change from his former good humor and friendliness, and it made me want to stay out of his way. Fortunately, I didn't see him that often. While we were cleaning cabins, he was usually down at the dock or tackle shop. Occasionally, we encountered him making a repair in a cabin we were cleaning or when we were down at the lake cleaning equipment. It was just a coldness I felt from him, but I was increasingly uneasy around him and, it seemed, he

around me.

CHAPTER 4

Fall 1999 - Spring 2003

High school was a socially awkward time for me. Charlie naturally drew people to her. Everyone liked her and wanted to be her friend. But things were different with me. Over the years my friends had fallen away, one by one, as their attention turned to boys and dating; topics that I found completely uninteresting. It seemed that with every passing day I was more alone. I felt isolated from other kids, first for my shyness, but as time went on, I knew there was something else set me apart, but I couldn't say exactly what or why.

Charlie and I were still best friends, but while Charlie had many friends, she was now my *only* friend. I looked to her to help me navigate those hard years. As best friends, we spent most of our time in one another's company. Sometimes we got together with other kids, but normally it was just the two of us. Neither of us dated. We even went to the Junior Prom together as best friends. Lots of girls went with other girls and many of the boys went that way too.

What we didn't realize was that Charlie's father had taken notice of just how much time we were spending together, and he was increasingly unhappy about it. He started to make comments to Charlie that she should spend less time with me, expand her circle of friends and start dating. It got uncomfortable enough that Charlie began avoiding him, like I was.

In the summer between our junior and senior years, Mr. Young decided it was time to take more direct action. He waited until a slow Thursday at the resort and asked Charlie to take a ride with him.

After they got back that afternoon, Charlie called me, "We need to talk. Can you meet me at the Buckeye?"

I texted back, "OK."

Charlie arrived at my house about 30 minutes later, motioning for us to go down to the Buckeye tree in my backyard. Every year from the minute the days began warming up, it was a good bet that at one time or another you could find us under the big branches of that huge, old tree. It was where we talked about things that were most private and important to us.

Once at the tree, Charlie seemed hesitant to begin. I could see that she was upset. I could tell from her expression that something was wrong and she either didn't want to, or didn't know how to, tell me about it.

"Come on, what's wrong?" I encouraged her. Charlie's expression was bleak. My unease grew and I knew then that something was very wrong.

Charlie looked down at her feet. "You know how you can tell when your parents aren't pleased with something you've done, but they don't want to come right out and say it, so they sort of talk about a bunch of things and only get to their point after they've talked about everything else?" she blurted out in a single breath.

"You mean like you're doing now?" I asked worriedly.

Charlie nodded, dreading the conversation to come. She took a breath and said sadly, "My dad told me he's been thinking that you and I are spending too much time together. He says that I never talk about boys, who I might like to date or even just be friends with. He thinks it's because we're together so much, there's no room for anybody else. He says that I'm no longer a child and I need to think about expanding my circle of friends and looking to my future."

I could see that Charlie was nervous. She'd started pacing. The direction the conversation was taking alarmed me.

"Dad said that it wasn't natural for two girls our age to spend as much time together as we do. He told me it embarrassed him in front of his friends when we went to the Junior Prom together. He said his friends even mentioned it. He said he doesn't want to see me graduate from high school without ever dating a boy; that dating is what girls my age should do, not just hang out with one other *girl*. He said that people were starting to gossip about us, and it was going to get worse unless I showed an interest in people besides just you."

I wanted to say something, but my throat was suddenly too dry. I couldn't force out a word. Although we'd never openly talked about our relationship, I knew we both understood what he was talking about.

Charlie looked at the ground. I told Dad that there were plenty of boys I liked, but not for 'dating.' That seemed to make him even angrier! He asked me how I ever could meet boys I might like if I spent all my time with you." Now Charlie looked directly at me, "Do you think he's right? Do you think we spend too much time together? Do you think our relationship is wrong or "unnatural?""

I almost tripped over my feet as I jumped up and quickly closed the space between us. I put my arms around her and was finally able to swallow so that I could get some words out. "No! I absolutely do *not* think our relationship is wrong or unnatural! Don't listen to him Charlie. I don't want you to stop being my friend. We are best friends forever! We're going to have a great senior year, we're going to the Senior Prom together, and then we're going to go to Washington State University and be roommates there. We have it all planned out."

Charlie's eyes welled with tears as she continued, "I told him I didn't care what other people said...but Jory, I'm not strong like you." She looked into my eyes and said, "I *do* care what people say about me, about us. I don't want to lose you or stop being your friend, but what if my dad's right? I've never hung out with any boys except my brother. Maybe it's best for us to set aside some time for other people. Maybe, even date a little...I don't know!

You know what's odd? I hadn't really thought about any of this before. I was just happy."

"So, if you are happy with the way things are now and I'm happy too, then where is this coming from? Is this your father or *you* talking? Is it your father or *you* who wants you to spend more time with boys?"

This conversation was like falling out of a tree and having the wind knocked out of me. My chest felt tight and suddenly I was miserable. I didn't know what else to say. I felt like I might throw up.

One thing was for sure, I didn't want to spend less time with Charlie. I wanted more. Down deep, I already knew that boys would never interest me, and I sincerely believed Charlie felt the same way. We'd never talked about it, but I didn't think we'd needed to. It was one of those things that went without saying. Everything was perfect now, why did it have to change?

I thought if I looked directly into her eyes, I might find some hope. Perhaps I'd misunderstood. Seeking reassurance from her, I said, "I thought we were happy but maybe I was wrong."

Charlie's response left no room for misunderstanding. "Jory, I'm so sorry, but I think I might need to do this. I should see how I feel about spending time with other people, not just you. Wait, that didn't come out the way I meant it. I mean, I want to keep spending time with you, but I want to expand my circle to see if I'm missing out on something. Maybe I *do* need to date some boys. I can't stand the thought of people looking down on me, talking about us like we're doing something wrong. Can you understand?"

I could see from Charlie's face that she'd not come to talk about or strategize how to respond to her father. She'd come to tell me the way things were going to be from here on out. I wanted to grab her and shake her until the Charlie I knew somehow re-emerged. I thought for a moment that the girl in front of my eyes might not even *be* Charlie. The Charlie I knew would never say those things. She'd never turn her back on me. Something was terribly wrong, but I had no idea how to fix it.

In the end, all I could do is answer her question. "No, I don't understand *at all*." But I *did* understand. I understood that this was the beginning of the end of us and there was nothing I could do about it.

We didn't exactly stop being friends after that, but we spent *a lot* less time together. Even then, it was never just the two of us like it had been before. I knew I risked pushing her further away if I tried to hold on to what used to be. Once in a while, we saw a movie or went shopping, but it was always with other people. On those occasions, I pretended that everything was fine between us, but I couldn't get Charlie's words out of my head.

We still worked together every Saturday (and now some Sunday mornings) but instead of us hanging out together for the rest of the day, Charlie always had some place else she needed to be or something else she'd planned to do. Nothing was the same. Terse text messages replaced hours of talking on the phone every day. Gradually, even the "good night" texts we'd exchanged every night for years dwindled to nothing.

Charlie got her driver's license, and her parents gave her a three-year-old, red Toyota Camry. I'd sometimes see her driving down our road. Occasionally, she'd see me out in the yard and wave as she passed me on her way to or back from town. It's not that she never stopped; sometimes she did. But she no longer asked me to join her...and she always looked sad when we talked.

CHAPTER 5

Two months into our senior year, Charlie stopped me in the hallway on my way to lunch. She looked downcast. "I wanted you to hear it from me and not through the grapevine, Jory. I've started dating Brian Sellers. I'm sorry."

"Congrats," I lied. What I really wanted to say was, "Why him and not me?" Tears pricked my eyes, as I turned and walked quickly away, not wanting her to see I was hurt.

I guess it probably *was* great for Brian. It was somehow even worse for me, knowing that Brian actually was a great guy. A cross-country athlete, he was also smart, kind, and funny. That he was terrific didn't lessen the blow nor the intense jealousy I felt. He was taking Charlie further away from me. That jealousy was the last piece of evidence I needed to be sure that my feelings for her went way beyond friendship. I had wanted so much more. Instead, I had lost her.

Throughout my senior year I felt invisible and adrift. Not having any real friends except for Charlie, I buried myself in books, movies, and schoolwork. I joined the girls' cross-country team and volunteered to be a yearbook photographer so I wouldn't have to explain to everyone why Charlie and I didn't hang out anymore. I told everyone that I had to be at games, races, and events to get pictures for the yearbook, which left me little time for my old friend.

Being with Charlie as we cleaned cabins had also become difficult. The conversations that used to flow so naturally between us were now stilted and strained. Even worse, I noticed that on occasions, when her father was around, our conversations pivoted to her boyfriend, Brian, and her new friends. It was all just too painful for me. I needed somehow to put my world back together without her. I wasn't sure how, or if, I could pull that off. I didn't tell Charlie that, of course. The days of us sharing everything with one another were past.

Finally, I did what I probably should have done months before. I quit my job. I let Mrs. Young know that, with all my school obligations, I wouldn't be able to work at the resort any longer. It was a difficult conversation with a woman who had always been kind and supportive.

Mrs. Young looked at me as if she was trying to see what I wasn't saying. "I've noticed you aren't around so much anymore. I've missed you. Is anything wrong Jory?"

I wanted to scream to the heavens that *everything* was wrong, but what good would it do? Instead, I assured her that everything was fine. I just had a lot of obligations at school.

Mrs. Young regarded me doubtfully for a long moment, then said, "Well, I'll miss seeing you around here, but I understand school must come first. Charlie will be disappointed, too." I didn't argue, but I couldn't agree. My silence grew awkward. I wanted to say more but couldn't. What might she think of me? I thanked her and headed back home, sadder than when I arrived.

Of the few doors left open between Charlie and me, another was now closed. It surprised me that Charlie called me later that day to try to talk me into staying. I knew I couldn't and shouldn't, and I didn't.

My mom knew something was eating at me. I knew she worried about me, and I could see that she was sad to see me so sad. She saw the distance widening between my best friend and me. She didn't understand it. But then, neither did I.

Both mom and Grandma encouraged me to talk with them about why I didn't see much of Charlie anymore, but I didn't have the words or courage to tell them about the feelings I had for her. I knew they both loved me, but would they turn away from me too, if they knew? Would they be embarrassed or ashamed of me like Jack was of Charlie? That terrifying, old specter of abandonment, the only gift I had ever received from my father, ensured my silence.

I held tight to the hope that once we graduated from high school, I would get another chance with Charlie and things might still turn around. We had decided years before that we would both go to the same college and be roommates. It had been a frequent topic of conversation when we studied brochures and statistics from various colleges. We'd finally agreed on Washington State University, located in the beautiful town of Pullman in eastern Washington state. Charlie wasn't sure what she wanted to major in yet, but she knew it would be something to do with literature or business. I already knew I wanted to be a science teacher. WSU had excellent programs in all three areas.

When I received my acceptance letter from WSU, along with a significant financial aid package, I couldn't wait to tell Charlie! I hadn't talked with her in several days. I excitedly punched in her number, hoping to hear that she'd received an acceptance letter too. When I told her my news, though, instead of the joyous squealing I had imagined, there was dead silence on her end of the phone.

"Charlie? Did you hear me? I got into the five-year Master of Teaching Program at WSU! Have you gotten a letter yet?"

There was still only silence on the other end of the call. Several seconds ticked by. Then Charlie burst into tears and, between sobs, admitted that she wouldn't be going to WSU. Instead, she would be attending the University of Southern California. She'd be more than 1,000 miles away from me for at least four years! All our years of dreaming together evaporated in that moment. I felt as if something inside of me shattered. I am pretty sure it was my heart.

I knew it was time for me to let go of my dreams of Charlie. I was heading to college now. I promised myself that I'd never again be caught up in a one-sided relationship or be foolish enough to hang onto someone who didn't want to be with me. And I would acknowledge that I was a lesbian from the start.

CHAPTER 6

Charlie and I stayed in touch off and on during college. The distance between us widened a little further when she texted me over the summer of her freshman year that she was going to begin using her full name, Charlotte. She had already changed her email address to reflect the new name, but she told me that I could still call her Charlie. As if she could ever be anything else to me.

Near the end of our sophomore year, Charlie texted me that she'd changed her mind about majors and was no longer thinking of pursuing an MBA in business. Instead, she'd decided to double major in English and secondary education. Because most of the credits would transfer over, she wouldn't have any trouble completing the new course work on her original timeline including her master's degree.

She now planned to become a high school English teacher. A few years ago, I would have been jumping up and down with excitement, hoping that we would get to teach together someday. Now, it seemed little more than a sign we still had some shared interests. I texted back, "Good choices," and left it at that.

In my junior year, I texted a picture of myself wearing my rainbow shirt at the Seattle Pride celebration. A few weeks later, I texted to tell her that I had been elected President of the Gay and Lesbian Caucus at WSU. She replied to both only with smiley faces.

By this time, I had accepted that Charlie and I would live our lives separately, and very differently. Charlie would likely never return to live in Mountain View. As far as I knew, she'd not been back at all since she left for college, not even for breaks. She was experiencing life on a much bigger canvas at USC in Los Angeles than was possible in Mountain View or Pullman. It was increasingly clear to me that her plans would center on building a life for herself in southern California. I, however, loved Mountain View and couldn't imagine living anywhere else. At 27,000 residents, I thought it was just the right size; large enough to have a lot to do, but small enough to retain some old-fashioned charm.

After graduation, I was hired into my dream job teaching Biology and Physics to 10th and 12th graders at Mountain View High School. I heard that Charlie was teaching English in Los Angeles.

We kept in touch via occasional Facebook posts and infrequent texts. I knew she was dating, but she hadn't said more than that. Then her Facebook posts began to include references to a fellow named Liam, until finally she mentioned him in nearly every post. He was a flight attendant, based out of LAX. A recent post included a picture of Charlie and Liam at a park. They were laughing at something that must have been happening behind the photographer. The caption said that they were, "moving in together."

I had assumed for some time that someday this would happen and had tried to prepare myself for it. I had thought about how I would feel and how I might respond. In my imagination, I would receive an email from Charlie announcing that she was moving in with, or was engaged to, Liam or someone else. I imagined I would be happy for her. I told myself that my feelings for Charlie were now nothing more than childhood memories. I would wish her the best and go on with my life. But I was wrong. It wasn't simple and I wasn't happy at all. Once again, I was devastated.

I felt demoralized and foolish as I relived every hammer blow to my heart from Charlie over the last six years. I vowed this time would be the last. As she'd made clear that summer before our senior year, Charlie's feelings toward me differed greatly from mine towards her. Continuing to believe otherwise was a waste of time and energy and could only lead to more grief. I was 24 years old, for heaven's sake. It was high time I start acting like an adult and make a life for myself.

Charlie, and my feelings for her, could no longer be a consideration. Since communication with Charlie often resulted in pain for me, I felt it was time I fully separated myself from her. I opened my computer and took a deep breath. I looked down to see my finger hovering over the keyboard. I hesitated for several moments, then blocked her from my Facebook page and unfriended her. Petty? Not really. I was not punishing Charlie; I was freeing myself. I just didn't want to know any more about her and her life with Liam or whoever. I had to move on.

CHAPTER 7

September 2010 - March 1, 2011

On a hot September afternoon, Charlie's world abruptly tilted when she answered the phone to hear her mother's tense voice. Charlie's father had suffered a debilitating stroke and her mom asked Charlie to come home right away. Charlie immediately requested personal leave to return to Mountain View. Using Liam's connections with the airlines, she was able to get a seat on a flight leaving for Boise early the next morning. Charlie asked Liam if he would take her to the airport, but he had his own flight to catch later that day so suggested she get an Uber. She packed for a week's stay, certain that things back home could be dealt with and put right in that amount of time.

The next day Charlie awakened early, left a note for Liam who was still asleep, and waited for the Uber to pick her up. She arrived at the airport with plenty of time to spare, printed out her ticket, checked her bag and headed for the TSA security check. She passed through the screener and made her way to the waiting area for her flight. Taking a seat where she could keep an eye on the jet-way door, she wondered for the hundredth time what she would find when she got home. How was her mother? Would her father even be alive? Would there be permanent damage from the stroke, and if so, to what extent? All questions that could not be answered yet and only served to increase her anxiety and guilt.

If only she'd lived closer. If only she'd visited her mom more often. If only she'd been more help. Instead, she'd taken for granted that her mother could take care of anything that came her way. Then there was her father. She'd promised herself that she'd never to return to Mountain View as long as he was there. And she'd kept that promise for nearly seven years. As her mind drifted to that day she made that promise, she explored the stomach-churning memories: the threats, rigid control and abuse that had polluted her relationship with him. Returning to Mountain View brought it all back as if it were yesterday.

When the passengers were called for boarding, Charlie fought an urge to turn around and walk out of the airport, as if not going home could change reality. Instead, she found her seat in the economy section and desperately hoped the man sitting next to her would not want to chat during the flight.

Charlie's mother, Adele, waited in Jack's room in the intensive care unit at Three Rivers Hospital and worried. Adele had notified her children of Jack's stroke and they were doing their best to get to Mountain View. Charlie would arrive this afternoon. Raylene, a wildlife biologist living in Billings, Montana, her husband Cliff, and four-year-old daughter Renee, were on their way by car and expected sometime Tuesday. Theo, an army officer currently deployed in Afghanistan, had requested compassionate leave. He hoped that it would be granted sometime within the next few days. However, for now, Adele was on her own. She was sitting next to Jack's bed hoping that her presence would help him feel less alone when she heard someone else enter the room. She looked up to see Tess Santos, Jory's mother, at the foot of the bed.

"Adele, I came as soon as I heard. How's Jack doing?" As Adele's face fell, Tess came around the bed and enveloped her in a warm hug. Adele found herself unable to contain the tears she had been fighting since she had first found Jack unconscious on the floor of the tackle shop. Tess quietly and firmly held Adele as sobs wracked her. Adele gradually brought herself under control and stepped back. She signaled that they step outside of the room to talk.

Once outside, Tess looked at Adele with concern. "How are you holding up?"

"Oh Tess, this is just awful. I seem to have no idea about anything right now. The doctors can't tell me the extent of the damage. Theo and Raylene are on their way. Even Charlie's coming home. She's flying into Boise, and I'm supposed to pick her up later this afternoon, but it doesn't feel quite right leaving Jack just now. Everything is still so tentative with his recovery. Having the kids here will help a lot, but none of them are here yet. Honestly Tess, right now I feel so alone." Tears overflowed her lower lashes as she spoke.

Tess squeezed Adele's hand. "I start my shift in less than an hour or I'd be happy to get Charlie. But I know that Jory's school is closed today for some sort of mold removal from the gym. I'll call her and see if she can pick Charlie up."

I saw the screen light up on my cell phone and my mother's name appear as I was vacuuming my already clean living-room rug. I grabbed the phone from the coffee table. Impressed with myself at getting to the phone before it went to voice mail, I answered, "Hey Mom, what's up?"

"I'm calling to ask a favor on behalf of Adele Young." Tess looked at Adele as she spoke. "Jack has had a stroke and isn't doing too well. The kids are all coming home. Charlie's flying into Boise at 1:30 today and needs to be picked up. Adele is waiting to see what the doctors have to say, and she doesn't feel right about leaving until she can talk with them. I'd be happy to get Charlie but I'm about to start a double shift covering for another nurse. I wondered if you could pick her up at the airport?"

The silence on my end was testament to my reluctance to spend any time around the woman who was once so important to me. It still hurt when I remembered how Charlie disappeared from my life. It had shattered me when she left Mountain View without even saying goodbye. I was surprised Mom would even ask this of me. Mom broke the silence and whispered sharply, "Adele has no one else to turn to right now, Jory."

I sighed as I thought about how Adele had been nothing but warm and supportive to me and my family. Now she needed my help. I could do that, and I should do that. I sighed deeply again before responding. "Sure, no problem, Mom. Give me the flight details."

CHAPTER 8

I had plenty of time, too much time really, to think during the 90-minute drive to Boise. As a young girl, I'd looked up to Jack Young, though that hadn't been the case for a long time. His actions had been the catalyst that destroyed my relationship with Charlie. But Charlie had responsibility in this as well. I didn't hold it against her that she wasn't strong enough to fight back against her father's narrow-mindedness when she was in high school and living in his house. She was just a child. But she'd been away from his control for years. She hadn't been a defenseless girl for a long time.

I also felt confused about Adele Young. The Mrs. Young that I knew was kind and generous. When we were working at the resort, she would often stop by to help Charlie and me finish our work at the cabins and then hand us the keys to a snowmobile or encourage us to take a canoe or kayak out on the lake while she finished up the last of the work on her own. She'd given me my first paying job.

However, if she knew what Jack had said to Charlie about our friendship, she'd done nothing to stop her husband's efforts to separate Charlie and me. But I didn't believe that to be true. I'd always thought that Mrs. Young didn't have any part in it and maybe was even unaware of Jack's actions. She deserved better of me than the hesitation I showed when she needed my help.

As for Charlie, I hadn't seen her in seven years nor heard from her at all in over a year. All I knew was from my grandma, who told me that she was still with Liam, living and working exactly where she once said she wanted to be: "A thousand miles away from Mountain View."

As I neared the airport, I could feel my anxiety rising. "Stop it!" I said to myself, "You are a grown woman fretting about things that you've put far behind. Be supportive. Just let Charlie lead any conversation. You don't have to say anything."

I parked in the short-term parking lot and walked inside the terminal. Boise had a beautiful, modern airport. The airiness provided by the skylights and tall glass walls eased my tension. The reader board flashed Charlie's flight and baggage carousel numbers. I hurried down to meet her in the baggage area. I'd only been waiting a few minutes when I spotted her as she came down the escalator. She looked tired and sad. That much, I had expected. What I hadn't expected was that she was also more beautiful, at least in my eyes, than I remembered. Her chestnut brown hair still brushed her shoulders and, as she stepped off the escalator, I could see that her eyes were that same hazel that could leave me feeling she could see right into me.

Those eyes widened in surprised at seeing me. I wasn't sure if I should hug her, shake her hand, or pat her on the shoulder. As I stood there indecisive, Charlie solved the problem by looking at me quizzically and enveloped me in a warm hug and stepped back after a moment. Her first words to me in years were a shocked, "Jory, what are you doing here?"

I felt confused by the hug, but I knew I needed to answer Charlie's question. I would have time to think about that hug later. So, I stepped back too and explained about my mother's call from the hospital and ended with "So, here I am."

Charlie smiled warmly and said, "Well, it's a nice surprise to see you. Thanks for coming."

I wasn't sure how to respond, so instead of the words I wished I could say, I just said, "Let's get your luggage," adding, "Do you need to use the restroom before we get on the highway?" She shook her head just as she spied her suitcase on the carousel. She grabbed it, and we were quickly out the door.

We didn't talk much until we were back on the highway headed toward Mountain View. I still wasn't sure what to say.

Did she want to be left alone with her thoughts, distracted by surface level conversation, or talk about her dad? I waited, wanting to let her make the first move and set the tone for our conversation on the ride home.

Finally, she looked at me. "Have you seen my father?"

"No, but my mom was at the hospital to see him. She said that he'd been asleep when she was there, but he didn't look like he was in any pain." I hesitantly added, "She did say that your mom looked tired and mentioned that your father seemed to have some paralysis on his left side."

We drove another 30 miles in silence. Charlie spent the entire time looking straight ahead. Finally, she managed to push out three words, "You blocked me."

"Hmm?" I said, uncertain of the context of her statement.

"You blocked me on Facebook. You unfriended me. Why, Jory?"

Startled, I struggled to explain. "I had to Charlie. You have Liam now. You had moved on with your life. I needed to do the same."

Turning to look at me, she asked, "Are you happy?"

I answered cautiously. "I have a good life in Mountain View, friends and family, and I love my job at the high school." It surprised me that I could condense my life into 20 words. And though what I had just told Charlie was the truth, it wasn't the full truth. My life was missing two ingredients essential to my long-term happiness. I knew that someday I wanted to share my life with a woman who loved me as deeply as I loved her and to have at least two children, three if I was completely honest. Well...and I didn't really have many friends and no really close friends. I'd always been so quiet and shy that friendships were difficult to initiate and maintain.

I elected to keep our conversation at the surface level, asking Charlie, "Tell me about where you live and your job." I stopped short of asking about Liam. A discussion of her love life would be too much for me. I am, after all, not a saint.

We chatted amiably for the next 40 minutes until we pulled into the hospital rotunda. "I'll take your bag up to the lodge and drop it off for you. If you need a ride anywhere or, really, if you need anything at all, call me. I still have the same phone number. Please, don't hesitate even for a second to call." Charlie smiled with genuine warmth, then recited my number in the sing-song tone I recognized from our childhood, "208-559-2210." She hadn't forgotten everything after all.

Within just a few days, Charlie knew her father's medical situation would not be resolved quickly. The stroke had caused widespread damage. Expecting her mom to be able handle everything at the resort by herself was just not realistic and leaving her mom alone to cope with everything on her own was something she'd never do. Charlie felt she had no choice. She contacted L.A. Unified School District to request to be released from her teaching contract and made plans to move home to Mountain View to help her mother run the resort, at least for the short term.

She sat down with her mother to discuss the life changes they were facing. Charlie explained that she would do anything to help her mother, but that willingness to help did not extend to helping her father directly. She would like to minimize contact with him. Adele's face fell and her eyes filled with tears as she heard this. Her eyes searched Charlie's and finally seemed to find the information she was seeking. She said simply," I understand, and I will do all I can to make that happen."

Charlie wondered, not for the first time, how much her mother really *did* understand. Did Adelle know about her husband's lies and intimidation? For that matter, had her father abused her mother too? They both knew this was a conversation long overdue.

Jack was released from the hospital and transferred for a six-week stay at a rehabilitation facility where he received specialized physical, occupational and speech therapies that would help him recover as much as possible. However, due to the extensive damage caused by the stroke, he hadn't progressed well. He could only speak a handful of words, and those unreliably, still couldn't walk on his own, and couldn't use his left arm. It had also affected his personality. He was more emotional, frequently crying, and easily frustrated and angered. Adele remained hopeful that, with time, he would regain some of what the stroke had taken. Charlie wondered if her mother's optimism was realistic.

Adele brought Jack home, arranging for a service to provide caregivers during the day. The ground floor mother-in-law apartment at the lodge accommodated the hospital bed and other appliances that were now necessary for Jack's daily care.

It wasn't surprising that I didn't see much of Charlie for the first two months of her stay in Mountain View. I knew from my grandma, who always seemed to know everything that was going on in our city, that Theo had been granted leave and had made it home to see his dad but had now returned to his unit in Afghanistan. Raylene who had been almost 8 months pregnant when Jack had his stroke was now not only back home in Montana but had also given birth to a baby girl who she named "Julia," after Adele's mother. Grandma had told me that Charlie had agreed to stay to help her mother get things back on track at the resort without Jack, I was surprised that she'd stayed this long. I knew her life was now in L.A.

Charlie had loved living in Los Angeles. The city was vibrant, open 24/7, warm year-round, and had fantastic shopping, museums, entertainment, and restaurants. She and Liam had a nice, if small, apartment in an older neighborhood only three miles from the school where Charlie taught and only one mile from the Metro Rail station.

To Liam, living in Los Angeles was an essential element of his life. He confessed to Charlie that as much as he loved her, he could not see himself leaving L.A. to help look after the resort, even for a short while. She was disappointed, but not surprised. Their life together was built on a few shared interests, an entertaining circle of friends and a passion for their jobs. They loved one another but loving someone differs greatly from being in love with that person.

Charlie and Liam's relationship had gone smoothly for almost two years. However, it was now becoming clear that it lacked the deep foundation of shared values and the willingness to compromise, even sacrifice, necessary to get through the challenging times that eventually confront every couple. The adjustments Charlie had to make because of Jack's stroke stressed their relationship to the breaking point.

Even so, they were both considerate people who didn't want to hurt one another. They decided to try to keep a long-distance relationship going until things settled down enough for Charlie to move back to L.A. They set up a schedule where Charlie flew down to L.A. for a long weekend on odd months and Liam up to Boise on even months. After just two months, the relationship was in deep trouble. Three months in, they agreed it was over.

Charlie felt unmoored. Moving back home again and living at the Lake was not something she'd ever wanted to do. The decision had totally upended her life, shattering all her plans. In the space of a few months, she'd lost her job, her home, and her boyfriend. She'd lost her father a long time ago.

Working together, Adele and Charlie were just able to keep things going. Adele had always managed the accommodations and business side of the resort. Jack had always handled the recreation side. He knew the summer and winter sports, maintained the recreational vehicles, boats and equipment, and was the resource for all guest questions ranging from the easiest hiking trails to the best lures or bait to catch lake trout. He also oversaw the care of the buildings and grounds. Charlie and Adele didn't have his expertise or experience. Running Clear Springs Lake Resort was overwhelming without Jack. Adele tried advertising for an experienced hand to fill the gap, but no suitable candidates had yet applied.

Adele and the kids made the decision to sell the resort. But that didn't solve the problem of finding someone to take over

Jack's responsibilities in the meantime—a challenge made even more difficult because the position would only be temporary until the resort closed.

In the end, it was Theo, with his military connections, who provided the solution. A sergeant in his company was retiring and was looking for something that would provide an income and keep him busy for the next six to nine months while he prepared to take off on a multi-year RV trip across the United States, Mexico, and Central America. It turned out to be an ideal match, and Adele was glad she'd found someone she could count on. It relieved a lot of the pressure on Adele and Charlie. Now they could concentrate on readying the resort so it would be at its best when the property was listed for sale.

Adele asked Charlie to lead the effort to find and interview realtors with the most experience in selling not just commercial property, but resort property similar to Clear Springs. After talking with three commercial realtors, they listed the property with Dave Fleming who worked out of Coeur d'Alene. He came highly recommended and had extensive experience with similar properties. Dave thought the resort would interest several buyers and was confident it would sell before the end of summer. On March 1st they listed the resort. The family knew that, to get the right price, they had to keep the resort open, in good shape and fully booked until they found new buyers.

CHAPTER 9

March 29, 2011

On a beautiful spring Wednesday in late March, just a few of weeks after the resort had been listed for sale, Charlie called me. I had just come home from the grocery store and was playing with Ernie, my plump orange tabby. I'd named him "Ernie" after my favorite sweet Muppet character who, like my cat, was always interested in investigating anything new. At the time of the call, Ernie was racing around the living room and bedroom, chasing, or perhaps being chased by, invisible enemies. I could not tell who the aggressor and Ernie was, fully engaged in an intense combat situation, wasn't interested in discussing it with me.

I heard my cell phone ring and glanced at the caller ID. I was astonished to see Charlie's name. I hesitated through the third ring and then accepted the call. "Hello," I answered tentatively. I heard only silence on the other end for several seconds. "Hello," I said again. Then finally, she spoke. Everything came out in two long, run-on sentences.

"Oh, Jory, I am so tired and sad, and everything is going wrong! I know I have no right to call you and you probably never wanted to hear from me again, but you said to call if I needed anything, and Jory, I really need someone to talk to. Would you mind...? Is it okay...? Please...? I mean, can I come over for a little while?"

I thought about how long I had hoped to hear words like this from Charlie. But now they didn't cause my heart to race or my hopes to leap. Now, I told myself, I felt only a sense of compassion for a woman who had lost so much, so quickly. Without any hesitation, I told her I would be home all evening and gave her my address. It seemed strange to think that she had never been to the house I had now owned for more than three years.

As I waited for Charlie, I tidied up my already tidy home. I took a bottle of wine out of the refrigerator and pulled two wine-glasses from the cupboard. I realized that I had no idea if Charlie preferred red or white or even if she liked wine, for that matter. When we were last together, we drank Coke or Dr. Pepper, too young to drink alcohol. Those thoughts steadied me, reminding me that the Charlie now on her way to my house was not the Charlie of my childhood. She was likely much different. And this visit was not about the "us" we had once been. This was all about Charlie.

I sliced some cheese, paired it with five-seed crackers and waited. Within 20 minutes, a car pulled up in front of my house. It wasn't her old red Toyota Camry, but the SUV that Jack had driven. Charlie sat in her car for several long minutes before I saw her open the driver's door and step out. At 5'5", she was two inches shorter than I, her body lithe and strong-looking. Just like at the airport, her beautiful, wavy, brown hair was down around her shoulders. She wore a bright blue blouse over beige capris and strappy sandals. She was everything I remembered and more.

I anxiously looked down at what I was wearing. I hadn't changed clothes from the sweatpants and WSU sweatshirt I put on that morning to clean the house. I began to lose a little confidence, then stopped. I reminded myself that this was not a date and how she thinks I look is no longer important to me. I knew I was not being honest with myself. I *did* care, but there was no time to change clothes now.

I opened the door to see the woman who I had once imagined spending my life with, standing on my front porch. Her eyes were a little red and puffy, evidence she had been crying. I took one step back to invite her into my house when she flew into my arms.

Oh my gosh! I closed my eyes and just held her. Holding

Charlie, she still felt as if she belonged there. Memories came crashing back, threatening to overwhelm me. I needed to step out of the embrace and put some distance between us. Before I could put that plan into action, I felt her shoulders shake and heard the unmistakable sounds of the deep sobbing that comes with great sorrow. Neither of us spoke as she cried loudly against my shoulder. In a minute that seemed like an hour, Charlie's sobs began to abate. As if by unspoken agreement, we gently dropped our arms, and I took a small step back as I reached out and took her hand. "Come on in and sit down with me, Charlie."

As Charlie moved toward the couch she said, "You know, only people in Mountain View still call me Charlie. When I went off to college, I left 'Charlie' here."

"Would you rather I call you Charlotte?" I asked, hoping my petulance didn't show.

"No! I've always preferred 'Charlie.' I just wanted to be different there."

I still didn't understand why she changed her name, but I was pleased that she wanted me to call her Charlie. It was a comfortable name and one that for years I was thrilled to hear on the other end of a phone call. I wondered what she would think if she knew that as children and even in my thoughts for the first few years after she pulled away from me, I always thought of her as "my Charlie." I reminded myself that those days were in the past and didn't mean much of anything now. This woman might still be Charlie, but for many years she had not been, "my Charlie."

"Oh, Jory, I am so mixed up! Mom accepted an offer on the resort. It was a good price, and we couldn't keep going the way we were, but it feels like I am losing that last thing in my life that I could count on always being there. My best memories are all tied up with the resort, my mom, and you. Now the resort will belong to someone else who will probably change everything, my mom will be moving to a new house, and you've blocked me on Facebook. Everything that was best in my life will have been completely wiped away." She hung her head and surrendered to tears.

This was far more painful for me than I had expected. These were not just Charlie's memories; they were mine also. I thought I would be the one to comfort her but found myself face to face with my own sense of profound loss and confusion.

Charlie took a moment to gather herself, then continued. "I've made so many bad decisions over the past seven years. I am so ashamed of the way I have treated you. I wasn't even sure if you would let me come over. How could I have made such a mess of everything, Jory?" Charlie dropped her hands into her lap and stared down at them.

I wasn't sure what to say or do. Should I just listen or was Charlie asking for help? My feelings toward Charlie were conflicted. I'd loved her. I'd been so angry. I'd felt so hurt. But there's was no way I would turn my back on someone who had once meant so much to me and who now seemed so despondent. I searched for words and hoped they would help.

"Clear Springs was your mom and dad's dream and they got to live it. You and Theo and Raylene got to live it too." Pointing out the positive aspects, I continued, "The sale of that dream will provide for your mom and dad for the rest of their lives."

"Jory, all of that is true. There are some things I want to forget here, but so many, many more I want to remember always. What if I begin to forget?"

I wondered if she was talking about me when she said there are things she wanted to forget. I used to be able to almost read her mind. Now I couldn't tell from her face or voice exactly what she meant. I guess that just showed how distant we had grown from one another.

Charlie was studying me. "Wait, you think I was talking about you when I said there were things I want to forget here, don't you?"

"I guess. Maybe. I don't know. It's been a long time, Charlie," I said softly.

"No! That is *not* what I meant! Yes, it has been a long time, but when I think of the best things about Mountain View, it's your face I see. I never wanted or meant to leave you. I wanted the same things you did. But I was afraid...and under duress."

I wanted to ask what she meant when she said she wanted the same things I did, that she'd been afraid, and under duress. Was it fear of being labeled a lesbian? Or did she mean she was afraid of her father? Or was it someone or something else? And what duress had she been under? I didn't know the answers to any of those questions and now did not seem like the time to start probing. I knew she was already upset and there was no need to escalate an already emotional situation. I wanted to make things easier for my childhood friend, not harder. Our growing-up years and any regrets were a long time ago.

I wondered if what might help Charlie would be to focus on something enjoyable rather than all she was worried she would or had already lost, something that would appeal to her creative side while easing her worries about forgetting the good times.

I could not help her erase bad memories: selling the resort, her father's condition, or whatever. But maybe I could help her find a way to ensure that she would not lose her good memories. An idea was forming in my mind that might help her do just that.

"I have an idea that might help keep you and your family's good memories preserved," I ventured. "What if you put together a Clear Lake Springs Resort photo history album?"

Charlie looked up, her curiosity piqued, so I continued to explain my idea. "You and your mom could start by taking pictures of some of the places and things at the resort that bring back memories of something fun or interesting that happened there. You could even get Theo and Raylene to tell you what pictures you could take for them. It could be a shared family activity or special event like a birthday or graduation, or just a funny story. You could add a few words describing what happened there. All of it could bound into an album and you could get copies made for everyone."

Frowning, Charlie said, "I'm not quite sure I'm following you. Tell me more."

"Okay. Well, you each jot down memories of happy or funny things that happened at the resort and where exactly they happened. One of you would take a picture capturing where the event occurred, then the person whose idea it was, writes a blurb describing what happened there. For example, remember when the whole Brookings family fell into the lake trying to grab the beer cooler that had fallen out of the canoe?" I looked at her with a raised brow. She nodded and smiled. "They were all screaming for help and Theo raced out in the Ski-Do to rescue them only to find out they were in only about two feet of water! You could take a picture of an empty canoe with a cooler floating beside it. Under it you would add Theo's description of the event."

Charlie chuckled at the memory. "That *was* funny. Mr. Brookings tried to blame Mrs. Brookings. She was having nothing of that and stormed back to their cabin with the beer, leaving sopping wet Mr. Brookings with their two sopping wet kids. Those kids were little monsters!"

I smiled at the memory, too. "When it's finished, the album will ensure the family's memories of the resort are never lost. Future generations can learn about their history from the pictures and stories. The only issue is that you probably want to get started right away before the sale closes and the new owners begin to change things around."

As I spoke, Charlie narrowed her eyes slightly and captured the right edge of her bottom lip between her teeth. I remembered that expression. It meant an idea intrigued her and she was thinking it through. I knew then that Charlie was going take this project on and find a hundred ways to improve it.

After some consideration, Charlie said, "You know, that might really be sort of therapeutic for all of us. I think it could be just what we need right now" Then more hesitantly, "I know that I have no right to ask this of you, but you are the only friend I have any more in Mountain View and you have so many memories of the resort, too. You remembered the Brookings incident," she laughed. "I had almost forgotten about that. Would you consider helping me get started with a few pictures?"

I felt the pull of Charlie's natural charm and it scared me. I just couldn't let myself go down that road again. I was all too aware of Charlie's power to draw me in. I didn't want to put myself in a vulnerable position where I would begin to think again how good we could be together.

She was here to help her mother through a particularly rough time of her life. When things settled down it was likely she would move back to L.A. to pick up where she'd left off. Our relationship, from the summer between our junior and senior years of high school and after had been completely one-sided. I was not going to let that happen again. I wanted to help her, but I also had to protect myself. Still, I felt harsh and unkind as I spoke my next words.

"I can come out to the lake to help you get started, but there is one condition. We need to agree to limit this to places and things your family will recognize and remember. It is your family's memory album." I felt I had to add, "I don't want to take pictures that remind only you and me of our friendship. I would rather not rehash those times. Is that going to be okay?"

I saw her expression fall and the light in her eyes dim. I knew that I had hurt her. The truth was this project would be just too painful for me to bear if it became about our shared memories. There was still so much that remained unresolved between us. I had been so deeply hurt and I knew I needed either to stay completely away from Charlie, as I had been doing the past couple of months, or make sure that when I was with her it would only be under tightly controlled conditions.

I silently vowed to protect myself from developing feelings toward her again. Despite the last few months, Charlie's home was no longer Mountain View. Eventually, she would return to Los Angeles or some other big city. And just like the last time, she would disappear from my life. This time, more than likely, forever.

The rest of our conversation was superficial, but it was what I needed, and I hoped it worked for Charlie, too. We talked about the sale of Clear Springs, my job at the high school, my mom and hers. We agreed to meet at the boat dock at 8:00 a.m. on Saturday to take the first photos.

I felt a little awkward as Charlie was leaving; neither of us seemed sure of how to say good-bye. Finally, I decided to fall back on our goodbye ritual when we were kids. I leaned in and gave her a chaste peck on the cheek and then stepped back. I reiterated that I would see her on Saturday. As she went out the door, I realized I hadn't remembered to offer her the wine and cheese.

I watched Charlie's car disappear around the corner, then gathered Ernie onto my lap and sat for a long time thinking about the past and what might have been. Jack Young's manipulation of Charlie that summer started an avalanche of events that changed the trajectory of our lives. I had often wondered if, in the intervening years, Charlie had even thought about me much. I'd had no reason to think so. But now, I wasn't so sure.

CHAPTER 10

April 2, 2011 - Morning

When I arrived at the resort on Saturday, I saw, once again, just how beautiful a place it was. The sun shone brightly, dancing on the deep blue water that carried the reflection of the lingering white snow on Mt. Washington in the distance. I hadn't been here in seven years, but the lodge, boat dock and tackle shop were just as I remembered them.

Charlie was sitting at the end of the dock with her legs hanging over the side, her feet not quite touching the water. As I grabbed my keys and daypack and headed down from the parking lot to join her, I noticed with pleasure that she had two cups of coffee by her side. As I stepped onto the dock, Charlie looked up at me with those warm hazel eyes that used to make my heart melt. We both had our hair tied back, mine gathered loosely at the nape of my neck and hers in a high ponytail. On the unseasonably warm day for early spring in northern Idaho, I had worn hiking shorts, while she wore denim shorts and we both wore sleeveless blouses. It reminded me of the days in grade and high school when we'd meet at the dock on our way to clean the cabins.

I tore my eyes away from her and reached down for a cup of the coffee she'd brought, glad to have something to occupy my hands. I spoke first. "Thanks for the coffee! Where is our first picture going to be?"

Charlie smiled that 250-watt smile of hers. "It's a beautiful day, so I was thinking the first photo could be from the top of the Summit Trail looking back down toward the resort and lake. Here's the story to go with it." Charlie turned toward the trail and the summit above. "The summit is where Theo proposed to Ursula. It was just before he was deployed. I wasn't here, but I've heard the story so often, I feel I was. Ursula thought they were just going on a fun all-day hike. Theo was so nervous that he was shaking as he and Ursula started toward the trailhead. When Ursula noticed Theo's hands were shaking, she thought he was coming down with the flu and wanted him to go back to the lodge to get some rest. He finally convinced her he'd just had too much coffee that morning.

"Theo called down to Mom when they were on their way back to say that Ursula had accepted. The two of them had enormous smiles on their faces when they caught sight of the family waiting to surprise them with bottles of champagne on ice. Everyone started clapping when Ursula held her hand aloft so that they could see her ring. I think this is going to be one of the best stories for the album."

I smiled at the story and nodded my agreement, "Sounds like a good choice."

We hefted our day packs, mine considerably fuller than Charlie's, and made our way to the trailhead. We paused to sign into the logbook before starting up the trail. The Summit Lookout Trail was an 8-mile round-trip hike that started on resort property and continued through state forest land. The first mile of the trail was maintained by the resort, and the trail was well groomed with hard-packed soil. The resort property line was just before the first look-out. We stopped at the first lookout to enjoy the panoramic view of the lake and resort. I took a couple of pictures with my phone. By agreement, Charlie had not brought hers. She was looking forward to several hours of uninterrupted hiking with no calls from the lodge for advice or guest issues.

From that point on, the trail got rougher as we entered the State Forest Service maintained portion of the hike. Hikers had to be careful to avoid turning an ankle or twisting a knee on this section. Still, it was safe enough for experienced hikers. Charlie and I had made this hike many times when we were younger. I was looking forward to the beauty of the mountains and the physical challenge of the 1,500 ft. elevation gain in the four miles to the summit.

With Charlie in the lead, we started up the trail at an easy pace. The forest was deep green with a mix of pine and fir trees that closed in around us so that we could see only a bit of the trail ahead and behind. A variety of birds could be heard but not seen in the dense growth. I recognized the call of a varied thrush somewhere above us. The sharp, sweet scent of pine brought with it a delicious sense of relief from our day-to-day cares. It was almost as if we had entered a different world, where our only concern was putting one foot in front of the other. Beneath the tall trees, there were occasional small clearings that sported miniature white snow drops in full bloom. I took in a deep breath, exhaled, and relaxed, glad that I lived in an area where these sights and smells were commonplace.

The trail's condition improved as we climbed, an indication that fewer hikers were using the trail as it continued its up-hill trajectory. We made good time to the second lookout one and three quarters miles from the first. The forest service had recently upgraded the safety barricades at the cliff edge at the lookouts to prevent hikers from straying too close to dangerous drop-offs. We stopped to take in the vista. From here, the forest appeared to go on forever, except for one spot off to the west that had burned several years ago as the result of a lightning strike. We took long drinks from our water bottles, looked at one another, nodded, and continued up the trail. The third lookout was only about a quarter mile away.

It took almost no time to reach the next lookout. From this point on, the trail, which had been following the edge of Deep Canyon, turned inland and upward toward the summit. We walked over and leaned against the newly installed railing to catch our breath and enjoy the sweeping scene of thousands of forested acres sprawling below. The metal of the railing was warm from the spring sun and felt good on our hands and arms. We could see all the way to the bottom of the canyon and the small stream that flowed there. The view was breathtaking.

We had been standing there for a couple of minutes when I heard a loud *CRACK!* Suddenly we were both falling in a hail of dirt, rocks, leaves, and branches. It happened so fast I had no time to be terrified. I knew it was a long way down and there was little chance that we could stop ourselves before we reached the bottom of the canyon. Abruptly, I slammed into solid rock. The landing took the breath out of me and my head was swimming. Everything went black for a second. It took me a minute to be able to breathe and realize I was still alive. My head and knee were throbbing from hitting rocks and roots on the way down. I had landed on rock ledge that was about 8 feet across and 4 feet deep at its widest point, tapering a little at both ends. It seemed solid enough.

Frantically, I looked around for Charlie. I hadn't been looking in her direction when the lookout collapsed, and I only had a sense that she was falling too. I was pretty sure she'd plunged down ahead of me, but I couldn't see any sign of her. I couldn't bring myself to look over the edge of the ledge for fear I would see her lying at the bottom of the canyon. I was dizzy and a little nauseous. I couldn't think straight.

Where was Charlie? Oh, God! Please let her still be alive! I started crying. Then I slowly realized I was hearing her calling my name, not from below me but higher up on the canyon wall. Still disoriented, I had trouble figuring out how she could be above me. My vision was blurry, but I finally saw her. She was upright, flat against the canyon wall about six feet down from where we had been standing and about five feet above me. As she had slid downward, she'd managed to stop her fall by grabbing hold of a thick root protruding from the canyon wall. I could see that her right leg was bleeding, and her face and arm were scraped pretty badly, but she was alive, and I was not alone. I took a moment to heartfully thank every deity I could think of.

As if I was not already scared enough, just then a small torrent of soil, roots and leaves cascaded down the hillside on the other side of the ledge, a reminder of how precarious our positions really were.

"Charlie? Charlie, can you hear me? Are you okay?" I cried out. The pain caused by raising my voice, even just a little, was like being hit in the head with a hammer. But I will never in my life forget how jubilant I was when I heard Charlie answer in a shaky voice, "I think I am. Some parts of me really hurt. But I don't think anything is broken. But, Jory, I don't think I can hold on much longer!"

I had to quickly figure out the best way to get her down to the relative safety of the rock shelf. I had always been at my best in an emergency. When others panicked or went to pieces, I became calm and could think clearly. I felt that calm descend on me now, pushing away some of the dizziness.

"Okay, Okay," I called back. "I've got you, Charlie. You are just a few feet above the ledge that stopped my fall. It's sturdy and it's pretty wide. It's safe here and there's room for both of us. Can you see me?"

"Yes!" She answered, moving her eyes in my direction but not her head.

"I am going to stand up and move over so that I am directly below you. Here is what you need to do. Keep holding the root as long as you can, slowly straighten out first your feet, and then your legs. Point your body as much as possible directly toward where I am standing. When I see you are in the best position, I will tell you to let go of the root and you will slide right into my arms. I am only a little way below you and this ledge is wide. You just need to aim your body at me. I will catch you as you slide down and we will both drop down onto the ledge. Charlie, can you do that?"

Failing to hear a response, I gentled my voice, "Charlie, can you do that?"

Charlie's voice shook as she finally responded. "It looks like more than a few feet to me."

"It's not."

"I'm scared, Jory."

"Don't be."

"Are you sure you can catch me?"

"Absolutely! There's nothing to this. It's no different from when we pretended to be gymnasts during the Atlanta Olympics. Remember, I always spotted for you when you were on the high bar? We've practiced for this moment, Charlie. Just like Atlanta."

I knew how hard it was to take information in when scared. I needed to make sure that she knew what I was asking her to do. So, I repeated my instructions. "First relax the muscles in your feet and legs and let them extend as far down as you can. Then allow them to slide toward me. As soon as I see your feet are as close as you can get to my arms, I will tell you to let go. Just slide down feet first. That's all you need to do. Let yourself slide into my arms just as we did when we were practicing our gymnastics. You can do this Charlie. Start letting your feet and legs extend down. I am right below you. I won't let you fall. I caught you then and I'll catch you now. Trust me, Charlie."

I watched as Charlie's feet moved ever so slowly down toward me. I knew that with every movement, it would be harder for her to support her weight with just one arm. "You're doing great. You're already closer. Just keep coming." I could see her arm shaking and knew she couldn't hold on much longer. OK, you are close enough. Let go of the root and slide down into my arms. Trust me! Don't jump. Just led your body slide down to me. Do it now! Now, Charlie!" And then, without a word, she let go and dropped toward me.

There was nothing graceful about it. All I could manage was to break her fall and barely keep her on the ledge. We crashed down to the ledge together, landing with arms and legs entangled. We stayed that way for a minute or two giving thanks that we were alive and safe, at least for the time being.

When I recovered my voice, I tried to reassure Charlie. What I had asked her to do was terrifying, and she was still shaking. Had I been unsuccessful in catching her there was little that might have prevented her from plunging all the way to the bottom of the canyon. It took both trust and enormous courage for her to let go when I asked her to. After all these years, Charlie still trusted me.

I held her closely. "You're okay now. You're safe. Shhh. It's okay. The bad part is all over and we're okay." I repeated the words to calm and comfort her that I'd been taught in first aid training.

Charlie tried to get up, but I held her tighter and kept her from moving.

"Wait, let's just stay where we are for another minute to get our breathing and heart rates back to normal." She seemed grateful for the temporary reprieve. I know I was. The contact between us was calming. We had come nearer to death than I wanted to think about. I was still a little dizzy and queasy. This had been way too close a call.

After a couple of minutes passed, I talked her through our next steps. We needed to stay near the middle where the ledge was widest. "Charlie, you are pretty much on top of me. Try to raise yourself up a little and move slowly over to your left. Let's try to get disentangled without aggravating any injuries we might have. And Charlie, stick as close to the canyon wall as you can. I don't know how sturdy the outside edges of the shelf are." She slowly drew in a deep breath, held it, and carefully pulled herself up and away from me. She gasped and I could see that moving was causing her pain, but I wasn't yet sure where she was hurt. I knew that we were both, at the very least, banged up and bruised. I hoped there would be nothing more severe once we made a proper assessment.

"Now Charlie, can you scoot just a little closer to the middle of the ledge?" Charlie began to work her way toward the middle of the ledge.

"Hold it! You are perfect right there."

Since I was facing the canyon wall when Charlie let herself drop, I needed to turn myself around to be facing outward and I took my time doing it. I carefully moved one leg at a time until I too was facing outward. Then slid down with my back against the wall into a seated position on the ledge. Charlie repeated those steps, and we were once again relatively safe and comfortable. We both discovered some new cuts and bruises as we gingerly moved to sit next to one another.

I looked over at Charlie. "Okay, the hardest part is over."

Charlie looked up at the canyon rim. "Oh, my God, what do you think happened up there?" We both studied the gaping wound in the canyon wall where the look-out barrier used to be.

"Where's the railing?" Charlie asked.

I too wondered what had happened to the barricade railing we had been leaning on. If it had hit either of us as we tumbled downward, we would have been seriously injured or worse. I saw no reason to share that thought with Charlie. We needed to stay calm and assess our options, not scare one another to death.

I responded to Charlie's question with the first thing that came into my mind, "Maybe when the Forest Service drilled down to put the footings in for the railing, it led to soil erosion which eventually undercut the footings. Our weight may have been the last straw causing the whole thing to give way. Engineers will be able to tell. What I do know is that when we get out of here, I am going to be asking them that question." We both smiled shakily.

I was thankful for the basic first aid training required of all teachers. We both had a pretty good idea of how to address any injuries we might have.

"Before we do anything else, let's take a look at one another to see what we are dealing with damage-wise. I am going to start by looking you over, then you can check me over."

I began at the top of her head and moved down her entire body. I was looking for any signs of pain, swelling, punctures, cuts, or bruises. I thought it would be best to leave our shoes in place to act as a built-in bandage and splint should there be any damage to our feet.

We had both worn shorts and sleeveless blouses which had offered no protection for our exposed arms and lower legs. Charlie had a 4" long cut on her right arm, and a 3" gouge that was less deep on her right leg. Both of her hands were abraded; her right hand the worse of the two. Her legs were skinned up in some places and her blouse was torn and one shoulder was sore and raw.

Charlie had lost her daypack. I thought I could see it at the bottom of the canyon, but I was afraid to lean too far over the edge to be sure. I still had my pack, probably because I had secured both the shoulder and belt straps. It was a little worse for the fall, but it was intact. Reaching inside, I pulled out one completely full and one nearly two-thirds full water bottle, and my first aid kit.

I patched Charlie up the best I could with the limited supplies from the kit. I used one of the alcohol wipes in the kit to clean my hands, which were dirty after the fall. I used two others to gently wipe away the tiny rocks and dirt that were embedded in Charlie's injuries, and then dabbed some antiseptic cream onto the cuts. The alcohol wipes stung like fire but Charlie only grimaced. I realized that we both had some degree of shock as well. Thankfully, the cuts on Charlie's leg and arm had pretty much stopped bleeding. I cleaned the cuts and dabbed some of the antiseptic cream into them too. I used the kit's two biggest bandages to bring the edges of the cut on her leg together and wrapped the whole thing with self-adhesive gauze. I similarly treated the gouge on her arm. I had a small bottle of Tylenol in my pack and Charlie gratefully swallowed two tablets with a sip of our precious water.

When it was my turn, Charlie just as carefully tended to my cuts and scrapes using the alcohol wipes, applying antiseptic cream and band-aids. My left knee was sore where I had twisted it but there wasn't much we could do about that now. My most troubling injury was a large bump on the back of my head which was likely the cause of my slight dizziness, nausea and pounding headache. I swallowed a couple of Tylenol (safe even if there is a concussion) and hoped they would work quickly.

Overall, we had been amazingly lucky. We both felt better just having cleaned up our cuts and scrapes. We had things under control and were back in charge. Well…. except for being stuck on the side of the canyon wall.

We settled with our backs to the canyon wall, each of us taking some time to think about how lucky we had been. Charlie looked over at me. "Jory, thank you. You saved my life!"

"You would have done the same thing for me without a second thought." I felt tears well up in my eyes thinking about how close Charlie came to dying here today. "You don't have any idea how glad I am that you are sitting safely next to me right now," I said in a near whisper.

She turned to face me, and I could see her tears. She took both of my hands into her scraped-up hands and said, "I think I do." We stayed that way for a few moments before she withdrew her hands from mine. "I feel the same way. Jory, I want to talk with you about so many things…."

"Me too," I said, "but first we should sort out our situation. We need to see what resources we have and decide on a plan. Once that is done, I promise we can talk."

"Makes sense, and you're not likely to run off," Charlie said with a laugh.

I grinned back at her.

As the sun rose higher in the sky, I was feeling the first pangs of thirst prickle along my throat and mouth. "I think we should take an inventory of our supplies, so we know what we have to work with."

Charlie nodded in agreement. "Good idea. Does anyone know you were coming out to the resort today? Will anyone expect you to be showing up somewhere tonight or tomorrow?"

"The only one waiting for me is Ernie. However, being a cat, he won't be concerned until he runs out of food--and I filled his bowls with food and water just before I left. But come Monday morning, it will be a different story. The school will miss me and will come searching. How about you?"

"Same, but without the cat," Charlie replied smiling. "Mom might come looking for me at the cabin later this afternoon or tomorrow, but she'll probably just think I've gone out on errands. Most evenings, she stays in with dad. Monday, if I am not back at work at the lodge I'll be missed though. I did tell Mom that I was taking a hike up the summit trail and we signed in at the trailhead and didn't sign out, so anyone looking will know we are likely to be somewhere along the trail."

I sighed. "Well, it was only a matter of time until the good news ran out. It sounds like we might be here for a while. However, the days are long this time of year and it's the weekend. There will be more hikers out and a good chance that we'll hear them as they go past the lookout or notice the broken railing. It could even be today, but I think we'll have a better chance tomorrow. We didn't see anyone else on the way up today. Of course, they could have headed out before us, and we may hear them on their way down."

"I think it's a safe bet that we'll be found and hauled out of here no later than tomorrow late afternoon or early evening. So whatever supplies we have, I think we should plan to make them last until Sunday, say 6:00 pm." Charlie seemed to find my prediction reasonable and leaned back against the cliff wall.

"So, let's inventory our resources. Let's start with my daypack." I dragged it onto my lap. First, I pulled my cell phone from an outside pocket. I held it up so that Charlie could see the screen was cracked. It still had a 70% charge but no reception.

No surprise there. I looked at the screen a little closer and saw two things that did surprise me: 1) the clock on my phone was working; and 2) it was only a few minutes after noon. It seemed like it should be much later.

I moved to the main compartment of my pack and began to pull out each item, laying them out between us. We had:

2 Bottles of water, one full and the other half full
1 Lightweight windbreaker jacket
1 Space blanket
1 Small nylon tarp
1 Swiss Army knife
1 Whistle
1 Tiny SAS Survival Guide
2 Cheese sandwiches
1 Small baggie partially full of trail mix
2 Energy bars
1 Travel Pack of SPF 30 Sunblock wipes
1 Bic lighter
1 Travel packet of Kleenex
1 Stubby LED flashlight
1 Small sewing kit
1 Small roll of parachute cord
1 First aid kit

As I looked over the supplies neatly laid out, I felt satisfied and even optimistic that it included everything that we would need to keep us safe and reasonably comfortable until we could get help.

I turned toward Charlie to see her shoulders heaving. "What's wrong?"

When she turned toward me, I could see that she was crying. After a moment she asked, almost angrily "Do you realize how fortunate we are? She held up a hand with her thumb and fore-finger nearly touching. "We came this close to dying today. We wouldn't have been just *hurt*. No one survives a 200-foot fall!"

"Yes, I know exactly how lucky we were," I quietly replied.

"I've been thanking the heavens about every two minutes since we were saved by this ledge."

"There's something else," Charlie said sharply, her anger taking an unexpected turn. "I've been no help at all! First, you save me, then you've thought of and brought everything we need to hold on until we are rescued. And me? I have *nothing* to contribute. It's a good thing that it was *my* daypack that got lost and you somehow kept hold of yours. Do you know what *I* had in *my* pack?"

Knowing this was a rhetorical question, I remained quiet and waited for Charlie to continue.

She held up a hand and angrily ticked off, "A sandwich, some chips, one bottle of water, a hat, and a book! Even if I would've managed to hold on to my pack, what good would it have been?"

"Jory, you've always planned so carefully. When we were kids, I teased you about it so many times. Well, today I have been on the receiving end of that careful planning. I'm never going to tease you about planning or double-checking ever again. Thank-you, thank-you, thank-you!" She threw both of her arms around me.

Oh, Charlie, I thought sadly as I hugged her in return. Don't you remember? *You always* brought the sunshine. *I always* brought the umbrella. Everything was just as it should have been.

Uncomfortable with where my thoughts had begun to veer, I steered the conversation to a safer topic. "What do you say we split half of one of the sandwiches and an energy bar now, and have a little water? For dinner, we can split the second half of the sandwich with some of the trail mix." There was no argument.

The cheese sandwich tasted great, and a little food and water seemed to have cheered us up. The sun had warmed the sharp cheddar cheese so that it seemed to melt in my mouth and the crunchy cracked wheat bread had a pleasing nutty flavor. Even the sips of warm water were wonderful! Not that I had practical knowledge of such events, but near-death experiences apparently make one appreciate even the simplest things in life, small amounts of food and water being prime examples.

After lunch we each took one of the sunscreen wipes, and applied it carefully along our faces, necks, and arms, hoping for at least a little protection from the bright spring sunshine. I carefully slit open the plastic wrapping around the nylon tarp using the Swiss Army knife. I removed the nylon tarp from the packet and spread it out over our legs to protect them from the sun. Thinking we might find the wrapper useful for something later. I carefully folded it and put it back into the backpack. I looked up to see Charlie smiling at me. For what, I didn't know. However, I was encouraged to see that she was feeling better.

I transferred the whistle from the pack into my pocket, then carefully repacked our supplies. To prevent any chance that the pack could be accidentally knocked off the ledge, we tied it to a bit of root sticking out from the canyon wall behind us. All we had to do now was to listen for hikers on the trail above us and somehow get their attention.

CHAPTER 11

April 2, 2011 - Afternoon

Charlie looked at me in that intense way she had. I felt she could read my every thought. After a moment, she said, "We've done everything we can for the time being. It's time for us to talk about the last eight years. I have a lot of explaining to do and we have so much to clear up between us, don't we?"

And there it was. The possibility of answering questions that had haunted me for years, at first incessantly, then eventually tapering off until they were just part of the background noise of my life. Answers that had eluded me. This morning on the trail, I might have felt differently at that prospect, but the accident seemed to have altered the way I felt about a lot of things. Charlie was right. We'd been very, very lucky.

Thinking about what it would have been like to be sitting on this ledge alone or with Charlie badly hurt or dead, I suddenly felt overwhelmed with emotion. I couldn't stop myself. Maybe it was her words, maybe delayed shock, maybe how close we'd come to disaster, or maybe it was something I did not yet care to put a name to, but I burst into tears.

"I thought you were dead! I thought you had fallen all the way down. I thought I would never see or talk to you again." Charlie scooted closer to me and put her right arm around me. We sat that way for a long time. Quiet, together, but alone in our thoughts and memories. I looked down to see my hands were trembling and let the tears flow.

Finally, Charlie said, "I know just what you mean. It's a miracle that we weren't killed today. We both know the only thing that saved us was this ledge. It's made me think about a lot of things, but at the top of my list is how close I came to never being able to set things right between us. There is so much you don't know. I don't want to chance waiting a minute longer. I *have* to talk to you, Jory!"

As she spoke, I felt my stomach drop. Looking down at my hands, I thought about what might come next. Her words made me uneasy. Part of me wanted to hear what she had to say, but I also was hesitant to upset the tenuous balance in my life that had allowed me to be at least content, if not truly happy over the past few years.

I forced my eyes to meet hers and, with a jolt, I knew that she had somehow seen exactly what I had been thinking.

"Let's begin with high school and my father," she said with an almost hopeless tone in her voice.

Knowing that she would not be easily deterred, I settled myself as comfortably as possible on the rough stone ledge to hear what Charlie needed to tell me.

"My father was never an easy man to live with. As you know, he had his own ideas about things and when he made up his mind, there was no changing it. He was always harder on me than he was on Theo or Raylene. But things got worse around the 9th grade. He wanted to know about my boyfriends. At first, I just told him the truth, that I wasn't interested in boys. After a while he blamed you for that. In our sophomore year, he started questioning me about what we did when we were alone together. I told him that we talked and hiked and kayaked and cleaned cabins, but that wasn't what he wanted to know."

"It seems like from then on, whenever I was alone with him, he repeated the same litany. Why was I with you all the time and why wasn't I interested in dating boys? He always seemed to know just what to say to make me feel small. It made me feel ashamed of my feelings for you.

At first, I wasn't entirely sure in what way he thought our friendship was too close, but by our junior year, I had a pretty good idea. He never actually said the word 'lesbian,' but it became increasingly clear that was what was behind his questions. He told me that people were beginning to talk. I hated the idea of people gossiping about us. I could imagine how awful it would be in school if people thought we were having a lesbian affair. He told me that I could never belong to a church, work in any government job, or even travel to a lot of countries if I continued down the road I was headed--I could even be arrested, which really scared me. I didn't think we really would have been arrested, but the thought of being accused of a crime frightened me."

"When he found out that you and I were going to the Junior Prom together, he totally exploded. He shouted things like 'no daughter of his would date girls!' and on and on. My mother tried to explain that this was how a lot of kids went to the prom nowadays, but he wouldn't listen. Mom sent me out of the room after that, but I could still hear them arguing. Jory, I think maybe he hit her! That's what it sounded like, anyway. I ran back into the room, but mom was gone, and dad yelled at me to 'get out!' So, I did. I grabbed the car keys and drove over to your house to pick you up and we went to the prom."

Charlie's revelations were shocking, but pieces also started falling into place that made sense of Mr. Young's behavior. She'd never said a word to me about his anger over us going to the Junior Prom together. The thought that he might have hit Mrs. Young brought back the nausea I thought I had overcome after hitting my head in the fall.

I started to speak, but Charlie held up her hand. "Please. Wait. I should have told you all of this years ago. Fear, shame, and I guess the best word for it is 'despair' kept me from it. I want...no, I *need* to get this out while I still have the courage to do it. Then we can talk. I will answer every question you have. I promise."

As difficult as it was, rather than asking what seemed to be the hundred questions I had swirling around in my mind, I remained silent. I resolved to show Charlie that I was listening intently, without judgment.

I leaned into her, and she hugged me a little tighter, took a deep breath and continued. "Looking back on it, I would give *anything* for a do-over. I *wish* I had stood up to him. I *wish* I would have told my mother. I *wish* I would have told you. But I was just a girl. I couldn't defy my father. It's no excuse, but he was the adult. Part of me believed that he knew what was right and wrong. He kept telling me over and over that our friendship was wrong and that you would soon see it as well. He wanted me far away from you because he said you were a destructive influence. I tried to shut out his words and ignore what he called his 'guidance.' But he never let up."

Charlie paused and sighed deeply, then confessed, "I don't know why I didn't fight his accusations or him. If I had spoken to my mother *then*, things might have gone differently, but I knew he'd see it as an end run around his authority. I was already afraid of him and scared of what he might do if I talked to her. Pushing back and provoking him seemed...dangerous."

As I looked over at Charlie, I saw her eyes fill with tears. Through an emotion-filled voice, she forced out, "I'm sorry, Jory." Then she turned her face into my shoulder and wept.

I waited silently for her tears to abate. Reaching into my backpack I retrieved the partially full water bottle. There was so much I wanted to ask, but I would honor Charlie's request that she tell her story all the way through before I asked any questions. I leaned over, kissed her on the forehead and handed her the bottle. "Take a few sips of this. It will help." Charlie took a couple of swallows and then handed the bottle back to me. Sitting quietly, we watched the shadows lengthen along the canyon wall.

After a few minutes, Charlie sat up straighter and said firmly. "Okay, I'm ready. This is one of the parts I am most ashamed of."

OMG! I thought to myself. There's more? But I held my tongue.

CHAPTER 12

"The day I came to your house to say that I needed to see you less often, this is what actually happened:"

It was a cool spring morning. Mom, Dad, Theo, Raylene and I were all at the breakfast table taking about this and that, mainly what was working well at the resort and what needed to be done next, but also the usual talk about school and sports. Dad hadn't spoken to me at all that morning. Just before I excused myself from the table, he finally spoke up, "I need Charlie to go with me this morning to pick up some supplies for the tackle shop. We shouldn't be gone more than a few hours" I wasn't looking forward to spending the day with him, but it turned out even worse than I could have imagined.

A few miles out of town, he pulled the truck into a small pull-out on the side of the road. "It's time we had a little more serious talk, you and me," he said. "I've tried to guide you away from your unacceptable relationship with that girl. I have done my best to gently guide you back into normal behavior for a girl your age. I've allowed you time to see that the way you are heading is unnatural and shameful."

"Your behavior has embarrassed me. Everyone is starting to figure it out. I've seen the way people are beginning to look at me. I'm not going to wait for them to begin whispering behind my back. 'Look at Jack Young. He's the father of the deviant daughter.'"

"Since you have chosen to ignore my guidance, I'm not going to be asking you to do things differently any longer. From now on, I will be telling you what you can and cannot do, where you can and can't go, and who you can and can't spend time with. I am going to stop you from making any more bad decisions. I have tried the gentle hand

with you, and it has failed. Now you will experience the iron fist. If you fail to obey me in any way, I will take actions that will be painful for you, and you won't be suffering alone. This is the guidance I have been asking of you for the past three years. No more asking. These are now rules you will live with."

Then dad started laying out his rules. "Jory is not to come to the resort at all anymore except to clean the cabins, and she must leave as soon as the work was done. If you try to see that girl away from the resort, I will see to it that you don't leave the resort except to go directly to school and directly back home for the rest of this school year and the next."

"You will be allowed to meet with Jory one last time. At the meeting, you will tell her that the two of you need to quit spending so much time together, that you need to expand your circle of friends, and that you would be starting to date boys."

"If you don't stop seeing one another I will meet with Jory and her mother to make sure she understands the real nature of your friendship and why you are no longer welcome to be around Charlie. If, even after that, you continue to see one another, I will call the school and tell them that Jory is making unwanted advances toward you but is too afraid to report it for fear Jory will seek revenge.

Charlie was shocked, "Mom would never let you do all of that." Without warning, he grabbed Charlie by the back of her neck, forced her to bend over at the waist, and hit her hard on the back of her head, and said "Don't worry, the bruise wouldn't show." The blow stunned Charlie. Her nose was bleeding from the punch forcing her nose into her knee. she fumbled in my pocket for a Kleenex to stop the bleeding. All the while, he just looked out the front window. Finally, he turned, looked me directly in the eyes, and said, "If you say anything to your mother, 'the little taste of obedience' you just tasted will be nothing compared to what would come to you and your mother.'"

"When we get to the store, clean yourself up in the restroom, then go directly to the car and wait for me."

I felt sick. I wanted to walk away, get some air, some space, some perspective. But I had nowhere to go. I could barely force myself to sit still as Charlie's story unfolded. I knew Mr. Young could be judgmental and stubborn, but I had no idea he would go this far.

Charlie finished the awful tale with her head down. When she looked up, she noticed that I was staring angrily away from her. She must have misunderstood my anger was directed at Mr. Young and thought it was aimed at her. Her expression moved from sadness to uncertainty. I knew she wanted to get through her explanation without interruption, but I could not let that misunderstanding stand.

"Charlie, I am so sorry your father did that to you and so sad that you had to handle it on your own. *None of this, not one tiny bit, was your fault!* What he did is horrendous!

Charlie gratefully rushed to explain further. "I had no weapons to fight against him. Jory, by this point, I was terrified of him. I was sick at the thought of losing you and even more sickened to be forced to hurt you. But I no longer knew what he might do or say. He'd hit me and I was pretty sure he would hit me again if I pushed back. I was pretty sure he'd hit my mother before, so I had every reason to believe he would hit her again if I didn't do what he told me to. And I was afraid he might hurt you next.

I was 17 years old; he was my father; he'd taken away my option of going to my mom his threats to hurt her if I told her about what he had said that morning. I couldn't go to you because I knew he would carry out the threats he had made about what he would do if I told you what he had said. I had no idea who else I could go to for help. I was completely intimidated. I believed he meant every word he said. I gave in and did everything he demanded."

I was thankful Charlie paused for a moment which gave me a chance to take in all she was telling me. *I had been so wrong about everything! Charlie hadn't turned her back on me!* She hadn't chosen her new friends and Brian over me! She had tried to protect me. But once again, before I could formulate my words, she rushed on.

Hearing what happened that day was just as awful as I worried it might be when Charlie began her story. Suddenly, my throat was so dry that I thought I might choke. But before I could ask for the water bottle, Charlie continued, and her revelations went from bad to worse.

"When you and I stopped spending time together, I was miserable. The longer we were separated, the worse I felt. I had shared everything with you. You knew me better than anybody else. You made me feel like the person I wanted to be, and I was being forced to shun you.

"Jory, by that time I knew that my feelings for you were about something deeper than friendship. After that day, whenever I saw you, all I wanted to do was run to you and tell you everything. Then maybe you could help me fix things. But I was terrified that my dad would carry through on his threats. I felt I had to protect not just me, but you and mom too. The only way I could see to do that was to give in. I made the wrong decision and the pain it caused you was my fault. You were the brightest light in my universe, and I swept you out of my sky."

I could no longer remain quiet. The words exploded out of me, "Charlie, this was *not* your fault! *Not one thing* about it was your fault! It was *all* your father! How I wish I would have known."

I felt a white-hot anger toward Charlie's father. And where was her mother while all this was happening? Did she know what Mr. Young was doing? I found it hard to believe that Mrs. Young would have had any part in it, but how could she *not* have known? Was she being physically abused as well?

My mind flashed back to the day after the Junior Prom when Jack moved from the owners' suite into the mother-in-law apartment. The timing seemed curious, but now was not the moment for me to ask a lot of questions. Right now, I didn't need to make anything harder on Charlie. If she knew, she would tell me in her own time.

I needed a break, and I thought Charlie might appreciate one as well. I moved my arm around her. I wanted to reassure her, but I wasn't sure what to say. I fell back on a ritual from our childhood that I hoped she would both remember and might help to convey the words that were difficult for me to articulate. I pulled one of the water bottles and the trail mix from my pack. I separated the trail mix. into a little pile for each of us. While Charlie took a few sips of water, I moved all the M&Ms from my pile into hers. When Charlie handed the bottle back to me, she saw what I had done, her short bark of laughter, told me she understood what I was trying to communicate, just as she always had.

We sat back against the wall, deep in our own thoughts for a long while. It was quiet on the ledge. The wind was still. The only sounds were occasional screeches of a pair of Cooper's hawks circling above the forest top. It was otherworldly to be up so high I could look down on the birds. The sun continued to beat down on us. The scent of the fir and pine trees around us grew richer as the temperature rose. I was grateful for the SPF wipes and nylon tarp that protected us from the sun.

Like so many beautiful things, the forest on the valley floor below was also terrifying. We were looking down into the tops of trees way below us. All that was between us on the ledge and the tops of the trees were a few scrubby bushes and some stunted trees barely hanging on to the canyon wall beneath us. None of them seemed anchored well enough to stop a second fall. Our perch, while seemingly solid, was still precarious.

Charlie spoke quietly to me. "Jory, I know this has been a lot to take in, but I would like to finish while we are here together on this shelf where nobody else can overhear or interrupt us. Can I tell you the rest? I need to tell you what happened with college."

I honestly didn't think I could take in any else. I wished for more time to think through what I had just heard for the first time. Before I could tell her that, I found myself nodding for her to go on. The forlorn look on her face returned as she took up the story from where she had left off.

"As bad as it was at home with my father watching my every move, I knew it wouldn't last forever. You and I had only to get through our senior year. After that, we would be in college together and effectively out of his reach.

"But, when it came time to submit my college applications, I discovered he was way ahead of me. Of course, he knew we had planned go to Washington State University, but he told me that I had to apply to at least two other colleges, just in case. He picked out the other two schools. It was a lot of extra work to complete the applications, but it was worth it to have him stop hounding me. I was accepted at both the University of Southern California and San Diego State. I wondered why he chose two so far away, but it really didn't make any difference to me. I knew I would be going to WSU.

"A few days later when I returned home from school, my father was waiting for me with a letter in his hand. It was from Washington State. I knew it would be my acceptance letter and my route to freedom. He insisted I open it in his presence. I was shocked to read my application had been turned down!"

"I'd held on at home throughout my senior year doing everything my father asked, knowing that you and I would be at WSU together and everything would be okay then. Heartbroken, I looked up from the letter to see my father watching me, smirking. He admitted that he had removed my transcripts and essay from the WSU application packet to make sure I wouldn't get accepted. He'd sabotaged me and called it 'giving me more direct guidance.'"

Bile rose up in my throat. "Oh my God, Charlie," I moaned in sympathy.

"He outmaneuvered me at every turn. Jory, keeping us apart became a crusade for him, justifying his every action. He told me that mom and he would cover my tuition, books, room, and board, and give me an allowance only if I went USC. If I tried to get into WSU that year or any year after, or if I ever told anyone why I was not attending WSU, he wouldn't pay one cent of my college education and he 'would see that mom paid for my defiance and not just once.' I felt completely trapped. For the last six years, I had worked at the resort for half pay in exchange for my parents putting aside money for my college tuition and expenses, 'at the college of my choice.' It all turned out to be a lie.

"I was emotionally broken by what he'd done. That afternoon, when I told you I wouldn't be going to WSU after all, I knew I'd lost everything...you, WSU, all of it. It was the worst day of my life. He'd won a war I had never understood.

"The only power I had left was to shut my father out of my life. I vowed that I would never see, write, or talk to my father again and I kept that promise right up until the day mom asked me to come home to help her with the resort after his stroke.

"I tried to keep in touch with you in college. But I knew from your texts and emails that you were slipping away from me as you slowly gave up on us ever being together again. How could I blame you?

I should have just told you everything after I graduated from USC. I don't know why I didn't. I guess I just thought that it was too late. Everything you had seen and heard from me over the previous six years had reinforced the message that I no longer cared about you. I thought you would never forgive me...and why should you? I knew I was never coming back to Mountain View and that your life was here. I gave up."

We were both emotionally exhausted by the end of Charlie's account. I had a dull, throbbing headache and Charlie looked pale and heartsick from reliving such a painful part of her life. I was very clear on one thing. I knew exactly how important my next words and actions would be.

Yes, part of me wanted to shake her for not coming to me with her father's threats so we could have fought back. I wanted to yell and scream at the unfairness of it all. We had lost so much time. And none of it needed to have happened except for the actions of one person.

But I had another, even stronger urge. I wanted to grab her and never let her go again. I wanted to soothe away the hurt that her father had caused. I thought again about how close we'd come to losing one another forever today. Without overthinking it, I leaned over and pulled Charlie into the tightest hug possible, considering how sore we both were. Tucked into one another, I didn't care about the bruises and cuts I had everywhere, and apparently neither did she as we melted into one another. I breathed in the familiar fragrance of sweet lime and coconut; a scent I have always associated with my one love, my Charlie.

I realized something else. I had been wrong about everything! For years I had blamed Charlie when it was *all* Jack Young. What Jack had done was monstrous: the threats, intimidation, violence, all of it. Not a single action had been Charlie's choice. It was all what *Jack made her do.*

As I thought about everything Charlie had just revealed, I began to understand just how calculated and crippling Jack's actions had been. Today, a curtain had been pulled back, uncovering years of emotional and physical abuse. From now on, I would make certain the curtain stayed open.

Was all of this engineered to avoid his being *embarrassed* by having a daughter who was a lesbian? Could it be that simple? Was he worried that it would somehow detract from his standing in Mountain View? Was his keeping Charlie away from me in high school to make sure no one might guess her sexuality there? Then to get her away far enough away from Mountain View that no one would ever find out she was a lesbian. Was it all intentionally engineered to make her hate him enough that, once gone, she would never want to return? He had come so close.

He weakened her bond with her mother through lies, threats and abuse. He destroyed Charlie's relationship with her best friend under the guise of protecting her from disgrace and ensured that the girls wouldn't have a chance to put things right by sending Charlie to a college over 1,000 miles from Mountain view. He extorted her silence and convinced her over time that it was her own actions and thoughts that were shameful, not his. Poor Charlie, finally thinking she was renouncing Jack's control over her, had vowed never to return to Mountain View. His abuse had been so effective that Charlie would continue her exile on her own, believing she was fighting back. Had it worked out exactly as Jack had hoped? Did Jack rejoice?

I wanted to exact revenge. I wanted to hurt Jack as he had hurt Charlie. I wanted to demand answers from Jack. But that was no longer a possibility. Because of the stroke, Jack was now experiencing his own isolation, and it was impermeable and permanent. In the end, Jack hadn't won after all. Charlie was back and everyone, but Jack, would have a second chance. At that moment, I vowed to protect Charlie for the rest of my life, to never again allow anyone to hurt her, as Jack had done.

I wanted to say all these things to Charlie, but in a way that would help, not hurt her further. I needed to think how to share my thoughts and feelings, and where and when. I felt that a ledge over a 200-foot drop was not that time and place. We were both emotionally exhausted. I considered my conflicting feelings and assumptions, acknowledging how cruel Jack had been, but leaving aside the deeper pain that would no doubt result if we unpacked too much, too soon.

We could have kept talking for hours longer, except Charlie thought she heard voices on the trail. I quickly grabbed the whistle from my pocket and began blowing in three-short, three-long blasts, hoping the hikers would recognize the SOS pattern and come to investigate. A few minutes later we heard a man calling to us. "Is somebody down there?"

"Yes," Charlie yelled back. "The look-out gave way as we were standing on it. We are on a ledge about 10 feet below you. Don't come any closer as we don't know how stable the ground is up there."

"Ok. We'll stay well back. Are you hurt?"

"Were okay. Nothing serious."

"Can you stay where you are? Are you safe?"

"Well, it seems like it for now. It's a little uncomfortable, but we think we're okay. We have water and food."

"We're on our way back down now. We'll call for help as soon as we get cell phone reception. What are your names?"

"Charlie Young and Jory Santos. Could you please let Adele Young at the resort know what happened and that we're okay? She'll be at the lodge."

"Got it!"

"When you're able to call for help, can you also let them know that they'll need climbing equipment to get us back up top and perhaps a stretcher? One of us has a twisted knee and may not be able to make it down the trail."

"Do you want one of us to stay with you?"

"Thank you so much, but we're okay. If you could clearly mark our location some way, it might speed things up. You don't know how good it is to hear your voices!"

"Ok, let's make sure we've got it. Your names are Charlie Young and Jory Santos. We'll keep our eyes on our phones to find cell phone reception as soon as possible. When we do, we'll call 911 and tell them where you are and what happened. We'll also tell them they'll need climbing equipment to get you both off the ledge. One of you has a twisted knee and may need a stretcher. We will find Adele Young and let her know you are safe, and that Search and Rescue is on its way. Did I get it all?"

"Yes. Adele is the owner of the resort. Just ask at the front desk. Be sure to leave your names and telephone numbers. We owe you a drink after all of this!"

"Will do. We're a couple of hours from the resort. But we'll watch our phones for service. If we get service before we get all the way down, there might be time to get a team up here and get you out tonight. If not, it might be tomorrow morning. Can you stay warm through the night?"

"We have a light tarp and a space blanket and enough food and water to see us through. We might not be comfortable, but we'll be okay."

"Alright, we're on our way. See you soon for that drink."

"Thanks again! See you soon."

And with that Jory and Charlie were alone again.

Charlie looked at her watch. Unbelievably, it was only 3:30 in the afternoon. We might make it home tonight!

We smiled at one another and then I started laughing and didn't seem able to stop. I wasn't even sure what I was laughing at or about. Charlie soon joined in. We laughed until our eyes streamed and our cheeks ached. Every time we met one another's eyes, the laughter started all over again. As our laughter gradually subsided, Charlie leaned over and gently kissed me on the cheek. No words were needed.

When we caught our breaths once again, I asked Charlie if she was hungry.

"I can't believe I am thinking about eating, but I'm starving," said Charlie.

"Me too. So how about a little dinner? Even if we have to wait until morning for Search and Rescue to reach us, we'll be out of here before lunch so we can have a little more to eat now than we had originally planned on. How about half a sandwich each, half the trail-mix *and* splitting an energy bar? It will be a feast! We can even finish the first bottle of water, part of the second, and take a couple more Tylenol."

After dinner, which we made last a long time, we gathered the wrappings and put them into the empty baggie, to pack out when we were rescued.

CHAPTER 13

April 2, 2011 - Evening

While ever so thankful for the ledge, it was not the most comfortable place to sit, especially for as many hours as we'd been here. I noticed Charlie wriggling around trying to get into a more comfortable position on the rough and hard surface. I reached for the daypack and pulled out the space blanket. I partially unfolded it so we could both could sit on it and be a little more comfortable. Neither of us wanted to chance slipping off the ledge by standing up, so we slowly and carefully worked the blanket under us. The side of the ledge where Charlie was sitting was more rugged than my side. I passed the windbreaker over to her for additional cushioning. At first, she didn't want to take it, but her side of the shelf was quite a bit bumpier than mine. She finally agreed.

Once we got settled again, I asked, "Are you going to talk to your mother about all of this?"

Charlie responded in a thoughtful voice, "I'm going to talk to her about everything once things settle down. I have been wondering a lot about how safe she was from Dad all these years. I also want to know how much, if anything, Mom knew about what Dad did to me."

I'd wanted to ask Charlie another question since we started up the trail but wasn't sure how to bring it up. Now it seemed like it could be just a part of our ongoing catching up. I asked a lead-in question. "Do you know your mom's plans once the sale closes?"

"Well, you know Mom. She's agreed to stay on at the resort for a month to help the new owners get the hang of it, but she's already started looking around for a new place. Mom feels like she should keep Dad with her. But he's getting so aggressive, I don't think it's safe for her anymore, if it ever was. I'm trying to get her to look for a care facility that's better equipped to deal with patients like Dad."

"Hey, is she working with a realtor?" I veered off the topic hoping to move to something lighter.

Charlie smiled. "Yes, of course she is. Guess who?"

"Would it by any chance be my Aunt Rose?"

"Yes," Charlie delightedly confirmed.

We both laughed remembering the many times Aunt Rose was a co-conspirator in some of our many adventures and pranks. Our moms would have grounded us for a month had they known what we were up to.

Charlie sputtered out through her laughter, "Remember the cigar and poker party, and the time we put the goat in your mom's garage, and that time we skipped school to go on the riverboat cruise pretending that we and Aunt Rose were dance hall girls from the 1850's? It took us weeks to save up for that cruise!"

Grinning, I replied, "I bet we visited every thrift shop in town two or three times to find just the right clothes for our outfits. It was worth every penny. We had so much fun! Aunt Rose still has the pictures from that cruise."

"Oh my gosh, what made us think those were good ideas and why would Aunt Rose go along with them?" Charlie asked.

"Because they *were* good ideas, I confirmed. And fun. Aunt Rose is all about fun! Nobody got hurt, and we got to stretch our wings a little without having to have an adult watching over us the whole time." I paused, then slowly drawled, "Wait, a minute, Aunt Rose *was* an adult. So, technically, we did have an adult watching over us the whole time!"

Charlie laughed. "It sure didn't seem like it, though. She had as much fun as we did."

An idea suddenly crept into my reminiscing "No...You don't

think...Do you suppose that Aunt Rose didn't keep our adventures a secret at all and our moms knew what we were up to all along?"

It all clicked into place. We looked at one another with big eyes and began to laugh again. We laughed and laughed at this new insight and how well we had once again been played by the women in our families.

Suddenly the years fell away. Sitting next to me was not the 26-year-old woman of today, but the 13-year-old Charlie I remembered dressed in the finery of her dance hall girl outfit. It made the moment even sweeter. We were best friends again, giggling and conspiring. It emboldened me to ask the question.

Trying to sound nonchalant, as if my next question was not vitally important to me, I asked, "Helping your mom through all the transitions she has planned sounds like it might take some time. Are you planning to stick around for a while?"

Charlie looked straight into my eyes as if her answer was as important to her as it was to me. "There's nothing much in L.A. for me to go back to, that's for sure. I don't have a job waiting. I didn't have much accumulated leave, so I requested to be released from my contract with L.A. Unified School District. I left my car with one of the teachers I worked with until I could get back to pick it up. Everything I wanted from the apartment is in storage. Liam and I let the apartment go, and I don't think I'd want to live there again even if we'd kept it."

At this news, my hopes that Charlie would stay in Idaho grew. Her next words confirmed it. "I was thinking of staying for a while to help Mom get all set up. I won't live in the same house as my father, so once I move out of the cabin, I'll need a place of my own for at least a few months, maybe longer depending on how things go. Oh, and I'll need a job. Charlie tossed off the last comment as if she were making a shopping list for groceries."

I knew she could easily get a job substitute teaching at my school. "I have an idea about a short-term job you might want to consider."

"Tell me," Charlie said, giving me her full attention.

"Well, you could consider substitute teaching. We're always short of substitutes at MVHS and at the middle school, too. With a master's degree you can substitute teach in Idaho without a teaching license. It's just a matter of taking an on-line orientation class, exam, and passing a background check. That takes only a few days. With your education and experience, I'm sure you'd qualify for the priority sub list...so, you would be among the first called for subbing assignments. You could be subbing in two weeks, maybe less."

I didn't want it to sound as if I were moving too fast, but I also wanted to help Charlie think about all her options. "Or if you wanted, you could apply for an Idaho teaching certificate based on your California license. Once you have that, you could look for part-time, or even full-time teaching which would get you much higher pay and benefits."

Charlie's eyes lit up with interest. "I like that idea. I *really* like that idea. I'll check it out on Monday. I think I might also give your Aunt Rose a call about apartments. I'm sure she'll have some good ideas and connections. I just might also ask her how much our moms knew about our secret adventures, too." She smiled warmly at the thought of it.

I wanted to tell her all I was thinking. I wanted her to stay longer in Mountain View. I wanted her to give us a chance for the relationship Jack had denied us. I wanted to tell her that once school was out for the year, there were summer school positions. I wanted to tell her that I had a pretty good idea that one of the English teachers at the high school was going to retire at the end of the year. But I didn't say any of those things. I needed time to think about everything Charlie had shared with me and to get to know adult-Charlie before I started to get my hopes up too high.

Not expecting rescuers for hours or even the next day, we couldn't have been more surprised when we heard a voice above us. "Charlie? Jory? We're with the Search and Rescue Unit of the Mountain View Fire Department. We're going to get you out of here and back into civilization."

It turned out that the hikers we'd talked to earlier had found that they had two bars of cell reception at the lookout just a quarter mile down the trail. They called 911 and the Fire Department took it from there. The Search and Rescue unit was on its way up the trail by 4:30 and at the look-out by 6:00. They didn't take any chances with my twisted knee and, to my great embarrassment, splinted it, wrapped it, and carted me down the mountain on a stretcher. We were back at the resort parking lot while a little light still remained in the night sky.

An ambulance was waiting at the parking lot nearest the trailhead and so was Adele Young. After we promised to see our doctors on Monday, we each signed waivers to decline transport to the hospital. We thanked the Fire Department rescue team profusely and promised to remember them at Christmas and, really, every holiday for the rest of our lives. We waived as they all packed up and headed back to town.

Adele had given both of us a quick hug on our return, then stood a little way apart while she waited for the Search and Rescue team to finish talking with us and reloading their equipment. Adele put her arms around Charlie and held her close. She surprised me by hugging me, too. "I am so relieved that you two are safe," she said, her eyes filling with tears. "How I have missed seeing you two together," she added wistfully.

"Jory, your mom and grandmother are inside. Let's go in where it's warmer and we can all sit down. We want to hear exactly what the troublesome-twosome has been up to this time." Charlie and I laughed when we heard Adele use her old nickname for the two of us.

I was a little hesitant about going into the lodge. Running into Jack tonight was on my list as one of the last things I would want to have happen. Charlie noticed my hesitation and said quietly, "Dad will be in bed by now." With that assurance, I joined Adele and Charlie as they walked into the lodge.

Mom looked us over and told Charlie she'd need to get the

deeper cut on her leg looked at by her doctor first thing in the morning, but she thought it wouldn't need stitches. When she looked at my knee, she advised me to keep it iced and elevated, rest it and see my doctor if it didn't improve over the next few days. Mom made sure our tetanus shots were current. For the rest, she admonished us to keep an eye out for infection or worsening pain, and then pronounced us otherwise in fair shape. After being cleared by Nurse Mom, we shared most of the details of our ordeal, omitting only the scariest and most personal parts. By 10:00 pm, the day was catching up with us. We both hurt all over. Everyone said goodnight to one another, and I promised to meet up with my family later that week.

CHAPTER 14

April 3 - 8, 2011

The day after our rescue was another warm and sunny spring day. A combination of aches and pains, dreams of falling, and thinking about all that Charlie had revealed made for a very poor night's rest. I finally fell into a dreamless sleep around 5:30 a.m. Ernie insisted that I get up at 8:30 because he was hungry. I didn't want to get up, but the cup of coffee that started my morning was, I swear, the best I'd ever tasted.

Around 9:00, my phone rang. It was Charlie. We talked for a long time about everything that had happened the day before and how lucky we were to be around to enjoy this morning. The conversation got much more serious as we revisited Charlie's revelations of the previous day. We still had a lot to talk about and we would no doubt return to this topic many more times. After a while, we moved on to lighter topics. Charlie filled me in on Theo's promotion, and Raylene's new baby. I filled her in on the goings on at the hospital where my mom works, and Aunt Rose's newest boyfriend.

Then her tone grew serious once again. "Jory, there is something else I want to tell you. I wanted to tell you this yesterday, but I didn't want it to get lost amongst the issues with my father. It's about Liam and me."

"Charlie, you don't have to…"

Uncharacteristically, Charlie interrupted me. "I *do* need to, Jory."

Still feeling overwhelmed from the previous day's revelations, I didn't think I had room in my brain for anything else. I wanted to think about what I'd heard yesterday before hearing any more.

At my hesitation, Charlie pleaded, "Please Jory. Please let me say this. These may be some of the most important words I've ever said."

"Okay, I'm listening," I said. I sat up straighter, my curiosity piqued, now prepared to listen intently.

Charlie began, "I didn't date much in college. Shortly after I graduated, I met Liam. He was different from other guys I knew. He was smart, funny, and always the life of the party. He had tons of stories about flights, passengers, and places he'd visited all over the world.

"We lived together for just over a year. Twice, he asked me to marry him. Both times I told him I wasn't ready. But that wasn't really the reason I didn't accept. It was because, while I really liked Liam, I didn't love him. I never had. I knew, deep down, he wasn't "the one." Then, when my father had his stroke, I saw a different side of Liam. After I came home to help at Clear Lake, he just sort of disappeared. He finally told me that family issues weren't something he wanted to deal with.

"Within two months of being back in Mountain View, I knew we weren't going to last. I couldn't stay in a relationship that only worked in the good times. It's not realistic to think you can have only sunny and never rainy days. We broke it off four months ago and we have only talked twice since then. They were amicable, but business-like conversations about the furniture and things in our apartment and cancelling our lease. He's a great guy and fun hang out with, but he would never be the partner I could imagine spending my life with.

"The last time I was in LA with Liam, I realized that the person I didn't want was standing right in front of me, while the person I really wanted was a thousand miles away."

Charlie cleared her throat and continued. "That person is you, Jory. It always has been. Then and now. You have always been "the one."

I didn't know what to say. Those were the words I had wished for so long to hear, but somehow, now, I felt confused...and scared. I needed to think. My thoughts were swirling...again.

Before I blurted out something I would probably regret, Charlie interrupted me again. "Wait, wait. Please, don't say anything now. For now, just think about what I have shared with you yesterday and today."

It was all I *had* been thinking about since yesterday and it would likely dominate my thoughts for a long time to come. But once again, before I had the words, she softly continued, "We'll have plenty of time to talk more once you've had a chance to consider everything. I know it all seems scary and uncertain right now, but promise me you'll think about everything I've told you?"

I tried to think what to say, but I was paralyzed. In the silence, I could hear Charlie breathing on the other end of the phone. She knew this would be difficult for me. She let the silence continue.

Once again, I was so disappointed in myself for not being able to say the words I so wanted to. Finally, I said, "I promise," managing to get at least that much out before my throat closed up.

After we said goodbye, I was left with a thousand thoughts careening through my mind.

I didn't see Charlie for the next few days. In a way, I was grateful because it gave me some time to think things through as I had promised her I would. She kept her word in giving me time to think, texting only to let me know what was going on at the resort and to report on her progress in getting the certificates and licenses that would allow her to teach in Mountain View.

As Adele worked on closing the sale, Charlie took full charge of running the lodge and cabins. She'd also agreed to arrange, oversee, and manage all the inspections and repairs that had to be finalized before escrow was complete. She was moving ahead on her personal plans, too. She'd read through the requirements for a substitute teaching certificate in Idaho and down-loaded the application packet to apply for a full teaching license. She had her hands full.

Adele had been tied up with CPAs for more than a week. It seemed as if she was constantly in meetings either with her own accountants or the buyers' accountants. The financial records of the resort were exhaustively studied to be sure that the representations about the assets, liabilities, rental history, and equipment depreciation were accurate. She and Jack had used Turner and Taylor as their CPAs for almost 20 years. She'd always secretly felt that T&T were too rigorous in the financial record-keeping procedures they insisted the Youngs follow, but it was certainly paying off now. Adele was confident that there would be few, if any, issues in the pre-closing audit. Still, the repeated discussions, questions, research, and resolution were nerve-wracking and time-consuming. In between, she was conferring with her lawyer, Oscar Juarez, negotiating the details of the sales contract agreement.

Despite things seemingly move along at breakneck speed, things moved even faster over the next week.

On Monday Charlie let me know that she had submitted her application for a substitute teaching certificate. Since there were relatively few requirements for subbing, it would be a short process and allow Charlie to start working and earning some income right away.

On Tuesday she texted that she'd taken the substitute teacher orientation class and exam on-line and was confident she'd passed. Once she had her substitute certificate, she'd be able to fill in for any absent teacher in grades seven through twelve. She'd also submitted her applications for an Idaho Teaching License which, she had been assured by the licensing clerk, would be fast tracked based on her current California License and master's degree.

On Wednesday, Charlie called to say that she'd received the results of her substitute teaching test and had, indeed, passed. Step one, complete!

In other good news, the buyers of Clear Springs Lake, Ron

and Cathy Cordova, signed-off on the final conditions of sale and accepted the inspection results, repairs, and accounting statements of the resort. The terms of the sale agreement had also been agreed on by both parties. The sale could now close as scheduled on April 26.

Charlie had originally promised Adele that she would stay in Mountain View until the resort was sold and Adele found a new home for herself and Jack. I knew I wanted more time with Charlie than that. Understanding that she had never wanted the separation Jack had forced upon her, I knew now that I wanted to see where a relationship between adult-Charlie an adult-Jory would go. Each day, and each step Charlie took to make it possible for her to stay a little longer in Mountain View was an affirmation that she wanted that too. She was methodically laying the groundwork to stay in Mountain View long term, and she was sharing every step and milestone with me along the way. My hopes soared as I read the text she sent later that afternoon.

I had been finishing up prepping my lessons for the following day when I heard the cheerful tone that alerted me to an incoming text message. Charlie had texted to say she had just completed the paperwork to have her car and household goods shipped from L.A. to Mountain View! All she had left to do was to provide the delivery address. She'd contacted Aunt Rose, and they were going apartment hunting the following Wednesday! I sedately walked over to my classroom door and carefully closed and locked it before high-fiving the air and launching into the world's happiest, happy dance! Charlie had just committed to staying in Mountain View!

I knew now that I wanted to give our relationship a real second chance. I also knew second chances are more tentative and would take time. Charlie's text meant that we would now have the time we needed to see where our relationship might lead. Each step Charlie had taken was further evidence to me that she'd meant every word she'd said that afternoon on the ledge. I felt like it was now my turn to show her that I was sincere, too.

As soon as I got home that afternoon and before I could over-think it, I grabbed my phone and called Charlie. "Hey Charlie," I said brightly, "I know you are busy with everything going on at the resort and getting licensed, but can you talk for a minute?"

"Of course."

"Well, two things. The first is to tell you how happy I was to get your text just now and I think you know why moving your car and furniture up here from L.A. would make me happy. The second is that I've been thinking a lot about everything you said last weekend. I want to talk with you about that some more. But I was also wondering if you would like to join me for dinner and a movie at my place this Saturday evening?"

There was a short silence, then she responded in a playful voice, "Why, Jory Santos, are you asking me out on a date?"

I swallowed at the flirty tone in her voice and responded in kind. "Why yes, I believe I am." I added hopefully, "I could pick you up around 6:00 if that works for you?"

"It's a date, 6:00 Saturday! And Jory?"

"Yes?"

"I can't wait!" Charlie said with delight in her voice.

Charlie and I were going on a date! In all the years we had known one another and all the time we had spent together, it had always been as friends, even though we both knew we were edging closer to something more. But this was an official date! A real date, and an acknowledgment of the pull we felt toward one another. A pull that went beyond friendship. This was a date! I had a huge smile on my face.

Somehow, while Charlie was still on the phone, I managed not to jump up and down with joy. As soon as we ended the call, my second happy dance of the day was something to behold. Thank goodness my only audience was Ernie. I tried to include him in the revelry, but Ernie turned out to be a terrible dance partner.

I spent the evening and next day thinking about our first date. I wanted it to be something special. It was time for us to stop concentrating on what drove us apart and turn our attention to what could bring us together. I tried to think of something that would remind Charlie of how much fun we had together once and how much fun we could have again. I had an idea. I grabbed paper and pencil. I planned everything out, then got to work.

Dinner and a movie made for the classic date. I wanted to start with dinner and then do something we had enjoyed doing together. I decided to try to find movies that we saw in our high school years. Thank goodness for the internet. I searched for "best movies of 2001 and 2002" and up popped a top 20 list. I looked through them and found two that were perfect choices. We had gone to see both movies when they played at the old Luxe Theater downtown: *Legally Blonde* in the summer of 2001 when we were 16, and *My Big Fat Greek Wedding* in April 2002. We'd loved those movies. I hoped they would rekindle happy memories for both of us. I checked to see if I could find them on cable. Sure enough, they both were streaming on Netflix.

The Luxe had closed a few years ago, but I remembered how much Charlie and I enjoyed going to the movies there and at the Orpheum, which was a little closer to our homes. These were both old-school theaters. Uniformed attendants sold tickets in a glass booth outside and similarly uniformed staff members collected tickets as movie-goers passed through the heavy double doors into the theater lobby. The floors were covered with thick, dark-patterned carpets. Heavy, floor-to-ceiling velvet curtains separated the foyer from the seating areas and blocked light from the auditorium. A large concession stand exuded the unmistakable aroma of buttery theater popcorn.

Concession stand treats were a big part of the experience of going to the theater. We always ordered the same snacks at every movie: a tub of hot, buttered popcorn, a big box of M&Ms, a large Coke to share, a straw for each of us, and extra napkins. As soon as we got our treats, we found our seats (always in the center of row five) and mixed the M&Ms with the popcorn in what we imagined to be our own secret recipe. Just thinking of M&M popcorn and Coke brought back such good memories that I decided I would have those on hand for our date on Saturday. My smile could have powered a small city. We have a date on Saturday!

I needed to plan what we were going to have for dinner. I wanted something that looked elegant but was quick and easy to prepare so I wouldn't be tied up in the kitchen all night. I decided on grilled salmon, roasted asparagus, and baked potatoes with butter, sour cream, and chives. For dessert we had M&M Popcorn and Coke. Perfect!

On Thursday evening, I called Charlie just to check in. We ended up talking for more than two hours. At first, our conversation revolved around thoughts and theories about Jack's actions and motivation, and then, by agreement, we turned away from the past. She shared how she and Adele were getting everything organized to turn the resort over to the Cordova's and Charlie's progress toward getting licensed to teach. I told her about my day at school, a problem student, and how, that morning, Ernie managed to get his head stuck in one of my shoes. Once we turned to current day events, it was just like old times.

Oh, and Charlie had resurrected another beloved tradition. Every single night since the summit hike, she'd sent me a good-night text. It may seem like a little thing, but it meant everything to me. It brought back the warm feelings of our younger days when Charlie never missed sending what she described as her "goodnight wishes to her best friend." I'd missed those more than I had allowed myself to realize. And of course, I had unblocked her from my phone and sent a friend request to her Facebook account.

CHAPTER 15

April 9, 2011

Saturday morning, I got everything ready for our date. As I dusted and vacuumed, I caught myself singing in a happy voice, "I've got a date with Char-lie." It was downright embarrassing, but I simply could not stop smiling.

Once my house was shining from top to bottom, I went to Jensen's Fish Market for fresh salmon filets, then to Kroger's for everything else. I added a bottle of good Pinot Gris to the cart, then picked up a second bottle on a whim. On my way home I stopped at the party store hoping to find a cardboard tub and the big paper cups and striped paper straws the Luxe theater had used for its popcorn and drinks. I was thrilled to find the store had them in stock. Now I had everything I needed!

Saturday seemed to simultaneously drag on and fly by. By 2:30 I had everything ready for dinner. At 3:30 I double-checked to make sure I could access both movies when the time came. At 3:45 I took a long shower and shampooed and conditioned my hair (twice) to bring out its luster. I put on a little mascara, blush, and a hint of taupe eyeshadow. I am not normally a painstaking dresser, but from 3:45 until 4:45 I tried on and then took off nearly every piece of clothing in my closet. I finally settled on a pair of black dress jeans that one of my fellow teachers said looked good on me. I paired it with an emerald sleeveless under-blouse with a metallic sheen and faint check. I finished the outfit with a white long-sleeved dress shirt. Since I only had few pairs of shoes, my footwear decision went a lot quicker.

All the arrangements were made, but I still had time to spare before I could drive over to get Charlie. I didn't know what to do with myself. I was so nervous. I so wanted this night to be just right. I wanted it to set the trajectory for our next steps.

I went into the living room to wait but couldn't sit still. I spent the next 30 minutes getting up, straightening a picture frame, sitting down, getting back up to plump the throw pillows on the couch, sitting back down, getting back up to be sure that all the clocks in the house showed the same time, sitting back down and repeat. From his vantage point on the arm of the couch, Ernie looked on as if watching a slow motion tennis game. He seemed to think I was losing.

When I left to pick up Charlie, I allowed plenty of time to ensure I wasn't late. I had to stop about a quarter mile up the road from the lodge to wait another 15 minutes so that I was not ridiculously early. I finally pulled into the resort parking lot at 5:55. I judged it to be a respectable arrival time, not too early but not late. Hopping out of my jeep, I made my way to the front door.

It surprised me how well I remembered the routines of the resort. I knew the front door to the lodge was always left open until early evening so that guests could come and go as they pleased during the day. At 7:00 the doors were locked; thereafter guests needed to use their room keys to enter. Since it wasn't quite 6:00, the door should still be open. I took a deep, calming breath, opened the door and stepped into the reception area.

Though I'd spent most of my time down at the cabins and docks when I worked at the resort, I'd been in the lodge hundreds of times. Looking around, I saw several changes from the last time I had been here. The reception desk was new, and the hardwood floors had been replaced with a rich hickory. Otherwise, the place looked much the same, but fresher, newer, and brighter.

Adele greeted me from behind the desk where she seemed to have been waiting for me. It brought back such strong and happy memories of the many times I met up with Charlie here. Adele looked up with a wide smile and eyes that seemed to twinkle as she looked into mine. "Hi Jory. Charlie will be right out. She is almost finished getting ready."

I wondered if Charlie had spent as much time getting ready for tonight as I had. From Adele's knowing smile and the Charlie I remembered, I judged it likely. Charlie had always taken care with how she dressed. Much more than I had. I smiled back at Adele as I thought of times in high school when Charlie had gently nudged me into putting on something a little different before we set off on one of our outings.

We looked at one another for a moment or two, trying to think what to say, when Adele solved the problem by coming around the reception desk and enveloping me in a warm embrace. "I am so happy to see you again, Jory," she said, pulling back to look at me, the smile remaining on her lips. I smiled back. I'd always liked Adele and seeing her now brought warm memories: my first real job, the times she had finished our work for us so that Charlie and I could get kayaks and go out onto the lake, and the many times the three of us had laughed at something that happened at the resort. She never failed to ask about my family.

"I've missed you too, Adele," I said, a little shy at addressing her by her first name. She had always been Mrs. Young to me as a girl.

"Let's make sure we set some time aside to catch up then. How are your mother, grandmother and aunt?"

We spent the next few minutes chatting with one another, until I caught site of Charlie as she came into the reception area and every word fell away. She was breathtaking! Her beautiful dark-brown hair shone under the chandelier and her eyes sparkled like the prisms in the light. Her smile nearly did me in. She was everything I had remembered and more. I could barely resist running to her and taking her into my arms at that very moment. I had spent so many days and nights dreaming of a moment like this. And right here, right now, it was happening. It was real! Years later than I had first imagined, but I would take it!

I think I might have *literally been stunned* by her. It would at least partially explain some of what happened next. As I greeted her, I tried to sound relaxed and not like the bundle of nerves I had somehow suddenly become.

"Hi Charlie," I said confidently, "it's great to sex you again." My eyes grew enormous. Horrified at my faux paus, I tried to correct myself but somehow my voice broke when I came to the bad word, "I mean, it's great to [*croak*] you again." Now desperate, I tried again. This time I managed to put a coherent sentence together. "Of course, what I meant to say was, it's great to *see* you again."

"Oh, no!" I thought. That little interchange could not have been more embarrassing! First, I stare at Charlie like some sort of pervert (and in front of her mother!), then I ask her to have sex with me like a horny adolescent boy, and then my voice cracks like one. I deeply wished that I could locate a switch to retract the floorboards so that I could fall through. No such luck.

I frantically looked around to see if I could find inspiration for a safer topic. Noticing again the new reception desk, I thought to comment on it. "I see you have a new reception breast." My eyes were now as big as saucers as I tried to correct again. "Reception desk! I meant reception desk!" I said in an overly loud voice.

I noticed with horror that Adele was studying me with obvious concern, and who could blame her! I looked to Charlie for help but saw that her hand was clamped tightly over her mouth, apparently trying to stifle...a scream?

I knew we had to get out of the lodge before I made it even worse. Charlie saved me as she hooked her arm through mine, bade her mom goodnight and gently nudged me toward the door, the location of which I had somehow forgotten. Where was that floor retracting switch, anyway?

The minute we made it into the Jeep, Charlie began to laugh out loud. It was totally contagious. Both of us laughing so hard we were bent over. When our laughter finally slowed a bit, she had only to say, "Good to sex you," and we were hysterical again.

Then we relived "reception breast" with a similar outcome. We laughed so hard that our cheeks and stomachs ached. It was a good long time before we calmed down enough for me to start the jeep and drive away.

Adele watched us through the window, waving hesitantly as we pulled out of the parking lot. She seemed to be smiling but goodness knows what she was thinking. I tried to keep myself from imagining the conversation between Adele and Charlie when she got home.

I managed to recover some of my poise by the time we arrived back at my house. Charlie took a careful look around the living room. It was decorated simply but I thought it looked and felt comfortable and welcoming. I didn't have much in the way of knick-knacks, but I did have two nice water colors on the wall painted by local artists. I had a large couch that faced a large screen TV mounted on the wall, a recliner that was my favorite place to read, and another comfortable chair that Ernie had claimed for himself. I thought it was simple and functional. Just like me.

I took Charlie's coat and was just hanging it up when she noticed Ernie. She'd always loved animals, but pets had never been an option at the lodge where guests might be allergic. As soon as she sat down, he jumped up into her lap. Charlie laughed with delight.

"Your cat likes me. What's his name?"

"I like you too, and his name is Ernie."

"Ernie, like the Muppet?"

"Exactly like Ernie the Muppet. That cute little Muppet is his namesake." I said smiling. "Would you like the grand tour of the house?" I offered.

"Of course!" Charlie replied, standing up and unseating Ernie.

It's a 20-year-old, three-bedroom, on just over two acres. It's more than I need but I fell in love with it the moment I saw it. It had been completely remodeled just three years before I bought it. it. The sellers were being transferred to Germany and wanted to get the house sold before they left the country. So, fortunately for me, they were willing to negotiate on price. And because it's surrounded by land zoned for agriculture, it feels very private.

I took Charlie through all the rooms in the house and even showed her the garage. We ended the tour in the large kitchen. It had stainless steel appliances, natural wood cabinetry and quartz counter tops with subtle blue marbling. An island in the center of the room served both as a breakfast bar and food prep station.

The wood grain tile on the kitchen floor mimicked the hardwood throughout the rest of the house. There were colorful rugs on the bedroom, guestroom and living room floors. From the kitchen, we walked out into the backyard, which consisted of a small deck, lawn and then pasture. "I hope to do so much more with the place one of these days. I'd like to expand the deck and add a large vegetable garden." Charlie took it all in, smiling.

"Are you getting hungry?" I asked Charlie.

"Famished."

"How do you feel about grilling the salmon, while I prepare the asparagus? I put the potatoes in to bake on my way to the lodge so they should be ready any time now."

"I love grilling," Charlie replied.

Charlie started the gas grill while I retrieved the salmon from the fridge. We worked together as if we had been doing it for years. In just a few minutes, dinner was ready. I plated the fish and sides while Charlie poured the Pinot Gris. As I set our plates on the island bar, I checked for Charlie's approval, "I thought we could just eat here rather than in the dining room. It's less formal." With her nod of agreement, we clinked glasses and sat down to dinner.

Our conversation was light and funny and comfortable. We continued to fill in the blanks in our histories with stories of what had happened in the previous seven years. I don't know if it was the seasoning or the cook, but the salmon was wonderful, and we both enjoyed the dinner. Only a little of the first bottle of wine remained. I was glad I'd thought to get a second.

After dinner Charlie cleared the table and I put the dishes in the dishwasher. I assigned corn-popping duties to Charlie while I finished cleaning up. When Charlie announced that the popcorn was ready, I told her I had a surprise and asked her to wait for me on the couch. As soon as she left the kitchen, I poured the popcorn into the bright red and yellow striped tub I'd kept hidden in the pantry, added a little melted butter so it would taste more like it did at the movies, then mixed in the M&Ms. I poured the Coke into the theater-sized cup and added two multi-colored straws. Smiling to myself, I put the popcorn and drink on the tray: it looked exactly like the treats at the Luxe!

Then I walked out, empty-handed, into the living room where Charlie was waiting for me. "Charlie, I have a special evening planned for you tonight and I want it to be a surprise. So, please close your eyes and don't open them until I ask you to."

Charlie nodded and closed her eyes.

Charlie wasn't one of those people who peeked when she was asked to keep her eyes closed. Like so much I remembered about her, Charlie loved surprises and would never intentionally ruin one by sneaking a look if she was asked not to.

I ran back to the kitchen and brought out the tray, placing it silently on the coffee table in front of Charlie. Sitting down next to her, I made sure my TV was set on mute as I cued up *Legally Blonde*.

When all was ready, I turned to Charlie. "Still keep your eyes closed until I tell you it's okay to open them."

Charlie nodded again.

I took her hand in mine and said, "I was hoping tonight you and I could pick up where we left off before Jack interfered. I thought a good place to begin would be in 2001 when we were 16. I wanted to remind us of those happy days. So...go back in time...remember the Luxe theater?

I watched the surprised smile form on Charlie's face, and with a little wiggle, she replied, "Of course. One of our two favorites."

Do you recall how cool those heavy curtains were that divided the foyer from the theater?"

"Yes," she affirmed.

"Remember how we always sat in the same place?"

Charlie's smile widened, as I could see almost see her picture the theater in her mind and nodded. "Yes, we always sat in the center of the 5th row"

"Do you remember what we always ordered from the concession stand?"

"Of course. Popcorn mixed with M&Ms and we shared a Coke."

"That's right." I loved that she had remembered. I knew then that I'd planned the perfect first date!

"Okay, now open your eyes."

Charlie saw the treats on the coffee table in front of her. Tears welled in her eyes, drawing answering tears from mine. "Now take a bite of our special popcorn and see if tastes as good as it used to, and if you still like it."

She took a small handful of the popcorn and M&M mix and tasted it. "Yum! It tastes exactly as I remember it and, yes, I still love it!"

I wanted to tell Charlie how happy I was to learn that she hadn't willingly turned her back on me, as I had believed for so many years. I wanted to somehow convey the many times I had thought of her since then and how much I hoped for a second chance at everything. The words in my head were always so much more articulate and compelling than I could ever force out of my mouth. But I desperately needed to share my thoughts, even if they didn't come out polished and perfect. So, I gave it a try. I had to count on Charlie remembering that I was better at doing, than saying.

"Charlie, I'm so happy we're together here tonight. I honestly don't have the words to describe how I feel, other than 'elated.' For so long, the best times of my life seemed to be behind me. Now, I feel the happiest times could be ahead. I'd love us to re-build our relationship. But let's remember that we're not start-ing over. We have a long history together. We go all the way back to the first day of second grade. Do you remember that day?"

"Yes!"

"We have that foundation to build on. On our very first official date, I want us to start by remembering the fun we had together back then. After tonight, I want us to work on making happy, fresh memories. It would be wonderful if you feel the same way."

"What you said, Jory. I want that too," she almost whispered.

"Okay then! I said delightedly. "Charlie Young, sit back, relax, and prepare to have a great evening. It's 2001. We're sophomores in high school. We're at the Luxe theater to see *Legally Blonde*. You told me then that this was one of your absolute favorites. Do you remember how much we laughed at that movie?"

Charlie actually squealed in delight, bringing a responding grin from me.

"Well, okay then, let's get started." I picked up the remote, ad-justed the volume and started the film.

We sat back and laughed at a movie that was as fun and funny today as it was ten years ago. As the movie played, both of us re-laxed into the sofa. She gradually scooted closer to me until our bodies were snuggled together. I smiled to myself remembering how we would sit just like that when we watched movies on the VHS tape player at my mom's house. We ate most of the popcorn and finished *Legally Blonde*. We talked about what we thought were the best scenes and what the funniest parts were.

Then it was time to move on to the second movie. I an-nounced with a flourish, "To complete tonight's entertainment, we will move along one more year to 2002. Next in our double feature presentation, we saw this movie when we were juniors. Do you remember, *My Big Fat Greek Wedding*? We had such a good time! Later we tried to learn the steps in the Greek wedding dance, remember? It was a lot less impressive with just two people."

Charlie looked at me with such a warm and affectionate expression, that now I was the one whose tears welled up...Apparently, we were both saps. To save myself from the embarrassment of crying like a baby, I quickly pressed "Start."

As the movie progressed and our laughter built, I reached over to hold Charlie's hand. She clasped mine in return and nestled even closer to me. As the closing credits flashed onto the screen, Charlie turned and kissed me gently on the lips. OMG!! I had dreamt of this moment. I had visualized what it would look like. I had imagined what it would feel like. But nothing, nothing I had imagined, came close to just how wonderful that kiss felt! Charlie's lips were soft and warm, and that kiss was literally the most wonderful feeling I had ever experienced. I leaned in and kissed her back, a bit more deeply. I hoped my kiss would mean as much to her as hers did to me. I also thought there was a real danger that those kisses just might cause the universe to tremble.

I wanted more, but instead I slowly pulled back. I didn't want to rush things. I wanted to go slow so we could both be sure we agreed about what was happening and where we were going. Honestly, I was scared and happy at the same time. Scared that I had let my defenses down. Happy to be so close to Charlie again. This was confusing! For the first time I fully understood why falling in love was often described as a roller coaster ride.

In the car, as I drove Charlie home, her hand found mine, and I gently rubbed her fingers with my thumb. At that moment, I thought I might actually die of happiness. When we pulled up to the lodge, Charlie leaned over and kissed me again. This time we both allowed the kiss to deepen before she gently pulled away. I could have happily stayed in that Jeep with Charlie all night. Too soon, she turned, opened her door, and stepped out onto the gravel parking lot. She turned back to say, "Thanks for the greatest first date ever!" and with a large smile and a small wave said, "See you soon!"

As she walked through the door to the lodge, I wondered how I would ever be able to sleep tonight. This whole evening, all of it: the dinner, the movies, the special popcorn, the closeness, the kisses. They all filled me with hope and would leave me walking on air for days. Our first date had been magical...well, except for the whole picking her up at the resort thing.

CHAPTER 16

April 10, 2011

The next day, Sunday, Charlie worked at the dock and tackle shop while I spent the morning playing with Ernie and grading lab reports from my 2nd and 5th period classes. The grading would have gone much quicker without Ernie's help. After reading and adding comments to each report, I separated them into three piles: 1) best, 2) passable, and 3) needs work. I would set time aside in the next week to give individual attention to the students whose papers "needed work."

Ernie delighted in running from some corner of the house and sliding into my carefully separated stacks. He completely obliterated my filing system. His disregard for my organization was annoying, but the resulting flurry of papers always made me laugh.

In the afternoon, I drove over to Mom's house to celebrate Aunt Rose's birthday. Aunt Rose, two years younger than Mom, would be turning 47 in two days, but today was one of the rare times that all of us could meet up at the same time. Mom and I had the day off, Grandma wasn't busy, and Aunt Rose scheduled her open house to end at 1:00, making it possible for all of us to get together later that day.

I was the last to arrive. As I let myself in and walked into the living room, I was greeted by the oddest sight. My Grandma, Mom and Aunt Rose were seated as if they were talking with one another, except they weren't. In fact, they all seemed to be silently staring at me, and not in a good way. I checked myself in the mirror above the fireplace to make sure I didn't have something stuck in my teeth and my hair was in place. All seemed in order. "What?" I asked defensively.

Grandma narrowed her eyes at me, then spoke first. "Weren't you supposed to get back to us after your near-disaster on the Summit Trail? That night, you told us all about the trail, the look-out collapsing and the rescue. You told us lots of things. But you entirely skipped what you and Charlie were doing on the trail in the first place." Mom, and Aunt Rose were nodding in agreement. "And don't think we didn't notice that you two kept looking at one another, either! We want to know what's going on. Now, give!"

I hesitated as I considered my options. Possible explanations flew through my mind but were rejected before the first word made it out of my mouth. Nothing sounded quite right. I had underestimated the observational skills of the two generations of Santos women in front of me. They had been lying in wait and now they were ready to pounce.

Stonewalling was clearly *not* a viable option. I caved. "Well, yes, I did say I would call you in day or so, but I got busy with school and helping Charlie find a job here in Mountain View…"

Before I could get the rest of my sentence out, six piercing eyes locked onto me again, but this time they were crinkled in smiles. All three of them spoke at once. Mom, looking delighted, said, "I always liked Charlie." Grandma, looking pleased, said, "You two were always something special." And Aunt Rose, looking mischievous, said, "Hot damn Jory, I wasn't sure you had it in you."

I realized that I had no hope of keeping my oh-so-very-tentative relationship with Charlie to myself. I came completely clean, sharing everything from her father's actions, to our forced separation, and to her likely moving to Mountain View. On a roll, I even told them we both were looking forward to seeing where our reacquaintance might lead.

They were shocked to hear about Jack's behavior and appalled at what Charlie had experienced at his hands. They made sure that I knew they wouldn't have given in to Jack's demands, nor flinched away from Charlie or me or our relationship. It was wonderful to know that they would have stood behind us. I took a moment to thank my lucky stars for the family I had. Quirky yes, nosy yes, opinionated always, but allies to the max. I knew how fortunate I was that they loved me unconditionally. And I loved them back.

The conversation moved to planning ways to welcome Charlie back to Mountain View and into our family group. Then, remembering that we were gathered this night to celebrate Rose's birthday, we moved into the kitchen for dinner and cake.

My mother made the best pot roast in Idaho, or maybe anywhere, and it was Aunt Rose's favorite meal. We put a good-sized dent in the roast and the chocolate chip birthday cake that came after. Everyone helped with the dishes and then all feelings of family solidarity were put aside as we came to back to our places at the table for a couple of hours of poker. Rose shuffled the deck, and we cut for the deal. Grandma drew a king which turned out to be the high card, picked up the deck and called the game, "Texas Hold 'em." The rest of us groaned. Grandma rocked at Texas Hold 'em. She ruthlessly and routinely cleaned every one of us out of all our change whenever we played. "Read'em and weep girls," she said, as she licked her thumb and doled out the cards. We continued until the mantel clock chimed 9:00, gathered our jackets and keys, thanked Mom for a fun evening and great meal, shared hugs all around, and headed off to our respective homes.

Once back at my house, richer in love but poorer from poker, I spent a few minutes with Ernie before setting up the coffee to brew automatically at 5:30, locking up the house, and climbing into bed. I read for about 30 minutes before I checked to make sure that my alarm clock was set and settled down to sleep.

I've had trust issues with alarm clocks since I was a kid. The faint worry that I might have forgotten to set the alarm nags at me, sometimes preventing me from getting to sleep and other times waking me up in the middle of the night. Sometimes both. Neither the fact that I always wake up before the alarm and hadn't overslept in 15 years, prevented me from worrying that I would oversleep the next morning.

I shook my head and laughed at my slightly irrational nightly double-checking ritual even as I sat back up and checked that the alarm was indeed set. I turned away from the now "for sure, times two" properly set alarm and looked down at my handsome orange tabby and explained, "Ernie, I know it might not make any sense to you, but I just have to be sure that my alarm is set." Ernie didn't even bother to look up from his catnip mouse. I've noticed that Ernie has yet to develop empathy.

I reached down to run my fingers through Ernie's soft fur. He tolerated my ministrations for a few strokes then trotted down toward the footboard where he dutifully curled up. He would keep my feet warm all night. With a contented sigh, I snapped off the bedside lamp. "Good night, Ernie." He remained silent.

The text message tone sounded almost immediately. I'd never been one to stay glued to my phone, but I had begun leaving it on my nightstand. I wanted to be sure I received Charlie's nightly message. I reached out, grabbed the phone, and checked the screen to see a message from Charlie. "Sleep tight, Jory." Smiling and feeling a little like a teenager, I answered in kind. Then put the phone back down and settled in for the night.

After a few minutes, I reached out from under the covers to re-check the alarm one last time.

CHAPTER 17

April 11 - 12, 2011

Spring weather in Northern Idaho is completely unpredictable. It can be blue sky and bright sun in the morning, and gloomy and rainy by early afternoon. Proving that point, on Monday morning I awoke, on time as usual, to the sound of wind and rain. I lay in bed listening to the rain tap at my window and tree branches scrape against the house. I pondered calling in sick and staying in bed all day, luxuriating in the soft sheets and cozy comforter. Instead, I forced myself out of bed and went to the window to see if the weather was as bad as it sounded.

I could see that we were in for a storm. The wind had already pruned many trees of their smallest and weakest branches and the lawn was covered with wet leaves that had been blown to the ground. Despite the weather, the enticing aroma of freshly brewed coffee drew me into the kitchen and the day itself.

Ninety minutes later I drove into the MVHS faculty parking lot and was pleased to see that my favorite parking spot, close to the door, was empty. A little thing, but it made me happy. Little things mean a lot. I shut off the engine of my Jeep. The Wrangler JK Unlimited was arguably the most versatile Jeep ever made, and perfect for Idaho's cold winters and hot summers, on-road or off. I truly loved that Jeep. It was a little battered, but so was I, and every dent and ding had a story.

Leaning over into the passenger seat, I collected my backpack and lunch, leaving my umbrella behind as it would be useless in the high winds that had added a sting to the pelting rain. I dashed for the big double doors at the front of the building. They were the only unlocked doors this early in the morning. I smiled as I entered and saw that a transformation had taken place. Early this morning, the upperclassmen had begun placing posters all along the halls advertising their proms. The competition between junior and senior proms was a school tradition. It was an integral part of prom season and had remained so for as long as anyone could remember.

On my way to my classroom, I stopped to fill my water bottle from the fountain. I was screwing the top back on when the trophy case next to the fountain caught my eye. The trophies of seniors rotated out every year right after graduation so that, at any one time, only the awards earned by the current student body were displayed. The top three shelves were filled with every team sport award earned over the past four years. The gold, silver and bronze trophies gleamed under the fluorescent hallway lights. The fourth shelf down was reserved for team academic awards. Even though students worked just as hard to prepare for and participate in academic competitions, those awards were mostly just paper certificates or ribbons, not shiny statues. The academic competitions never saw cheer leaders, broad attendance, or any type of recognition beyond a brief blurb in the school's newspaper. It simply was not right! I made a note to myself to bring up this inequity again at the next faculty senate meeting. What a mood I was in today!

I took a full 360-degree turn in the hallway. Despite the many things that bother me at my school, I truly love teaching here. My students come to me having learned the basics in earlier grades and it's my job to teach them how to use that knowledge to begin thinking for themselves. Sometimes what they come up with is interesting, sometimes hilarious, but most of the time what I see is a steady growth in their abilities to use reason to make decisions, to discern good science from bad, to see failure as a step toward success, and to understand that perseverance is the key to attaining worthwhile knowledge and skills. These skills will help make them good scientists and better adults. In my classes I set the bar high to keep my students aiming high and I support them in always doing their best. I believe they can excel and most all of them do. I work hard to make my classes interesting and challenging. I do my best to give my students a good experience every day.

Some days, time seems to creep but most days, time seems to fly. On the fly-by days, I glance at the clock to see how much time is left in the period, thinking we're just getting into the lesson, and am surprised to find just a few minutes left to go. Today was a fly-by day. I looked up and saw there were only five minutes before the bell. I had to hurry to close the lesson.

When the bell rang, the room quickly emptied as students hurried out to meet up with friends for lunch. The next 30 minutes were all mine. I checked my cell phone to discover that I had three missed calls from Charlie. Three calls in two hours worried me. I closed my classroom door for some privacy and called her back. She answered on the second ring. I could tell by her voice that something was very wrong.

"Thanks for calling back, Jory. Things are a mess here."

"What's happened?"

"Well, my father has really done it this time. He got frustrated and lost his temper with Doug, his caregiver. Apparently, Doug didn't get him his juice as quickly as he wanted. Anyway, Dad threw a paperweight at him and hit him in the chin. When Doug tried to calm him down, dad hit him again, this time with his fist. Mom heard the commotion and came running. It took the two of them a long time to finally get him quieted down.

"Mom called me to come over to the apartment. When I arrived, Doug was holding a wet towel to his face to stop the bleeding from the cut on his chin. I took a brief look at the cut and could tell it would need a stitch or two. We decided that I would take Doug to Urgent Care, while mom stayed at the lodge with Dad.

Doug, of course, had to notify the service to report that a patient had injured him, and he was on his way to Urgent Care. The service sent out a supervisor right away to meet with Doug at Urgent Care, then the supervisor came to the resort to talk to Mom.

He told her that Dad had reached a point where it wasn't safe for their staff to provide in-home care any longer and it wasn't safe for Mom either. He's right, Jory. He needs a greater degree of care that we can provide at the resort. Mom and I talked over our options and agreed that it's time for Dad to be placed in specialized residential care that's set up to deal with aggressive patients and where round-the-clock staff have the skills, medications, and resources to keep *everybody safe*."

"Mom feels terrible about what happened to Doug. He ended up having to get three stitches. Mom feels it's all her fault for keeping Dad at home for as long as she has."

I thought about what to say next. I settled on, "Sounds like an awful morning. Your poor mother. She must be shaken."

"She is. I'm so glad I'm here to help her. I can't imagine what it would be like for her if she had to go through this all by herself on top of everything else that's going on here."

"Is there anything I can do to help?" I offered. "With the sale of Clear Lake about to go through, and now this, I imagine Adele and you are stretched pretty thin. I still remember how to clean cabins and kayaks if that would help."

I could hear the smile in Charlie's voice when she replied. "If we need any emergency cleaning, you're our girl, Jory. Count on it. Until then, it really helps just to talk to you."

"Talking to you is a job that I'm happy to take on. What are you and your mom thinking of doing?"

"Well, the service will only agree to staffing Dad's care for one more week while we make other arrangements. They want to have two caregivers at a time on duty, which costs a lot more. But, of course, mom agreed. The service will have two new people over here by noon. They recommended Sunrise View as the best facility to handle Dad's multiple issues. That's the same place Dad's neurologist had suggested. So, we put a call in to Sunrise View and set up a time to meet tomorrow. If it turns out to be a good option, we'll figure out what to do from there."

"It sounds like you have a good plan. How about I bring over dinner for you two tonight?"

"Thanks, but I think we'll probably just stop at a restaurant on the way home. I sure do appreciate the offer though, and so will Mom."

"Will you call to let me know how things go tomorrow and what you find out from the care center?"

"Of course. You know, Jory, we all knew this day was coming. Now some hard decisions need to be made. Mom said that Dad was adamant about staying at home, but Dad's recent violent behavior has taken that option right off the table. I'm glad I'm here with mom and I'm glad you're here with me."

Charlie and I said our goodbyes.

During my prep period, I was just finishing putting the final touches to my lesson plan for the next week when Camille, my principal, stuck her head in the room.

"Hey Jory. Sorry to interrupt your planning but I wanted to get your any ideas or recommendations regarding good prospects to teach the 6-week summer school session this year. Frankly, we're nearly desperate for someone to teach the English and writing classes.

I immediately thought of Charlie. "I do have one or two ideas. How about if I nose around a little get back to you later this week?"

"That would be great, Jory, I appreciate any help you can give." And with that, she turned and was out the door, leaving my mind whirling with possibilities.

I hurried home that afternoon, eager to be somewhere I could speak freely to Charlie. She called just as I opened the front door. I put down my files, folders and bags and settled on the couch to give her my undivided attention. Our calls were rapidly becoming the high point of my days.

"I wanted to let you know that things have settled down this afternoon. The new caregivers have worked out well so far. Mom and I have an appointment with the administrator at Sunrise View tomorrow and we're both looking forward to meeting with her."

We talked for a few more minutes and then Charlie got called away to handle a problem a guest was having with his credit card.

As I walked into my bedroom to change out of my work clothes, I saw Ernie sitting in the middle of the bed looking oddly innocent. "How are you, baby?" I cooed. "Did you have a good day?" As I scratched him on his favorite spot just under his chin, I noticed a mostly unwound roll of toilet paper in the doorway between the bedroom and the bath. As I gathered up the white tissue streamers he'd left behind, I realized that, for him, it had been a very fun day indeed.

The next afternoon, Charlie and, to my surprise, her mother, called me. Adele started the conversation with an explanation. "Charlie and I have been working on arrangements for Jack all day and we think we have a decent plan. But before we call Theo and Raylene, we wanted to bounce it off someone else to see how it sounds. Charlie suggested we try you, and I thought it was a great idea. Do you mind going over this with us?"

"Of course, not," I said, using my warmest and most encouraging voice.

"Jory, please tell us if anything we say doesn't sound right or if we've left something out."

"Okay, I'm listening." I seated myself at the kitchen island and prepared to make some notes, if needed.

Charlie started off, "We met with Jocelyn Sanchez, the Director of Sunrise View this morning." There was a pause and I imagined Charlie nodding for her mother to continue.

Adele jumped in. "Neither one of us had ever been there before. Our first impressions were very positive. Jocelyn invited us into her office. She asked a lot of questions about Jack's condition and answered a lot of ours about Sunrise View. We were totally frank about what had just happened and what we knew about his medical conditions and prognoses.

"She asked what our priorities were for Jack's care. I told her that I wanted him to be safe and in the best possible environment given his needs. Jocelyn explained the challenges of balancing freedom with oversight for aggressive patients and explained the protocols Sunrise uses to minimize and de-escalate aggression. Honestly, the more she talked, the better I felt about everything.

"Jocelyn then invited us to tour the facility. We started with the resident rooms. All the rooms are on either side of the main hallway. Rooms on one side of the hall look out on a large deck with cheerful umbrellas, tables, and chairs. Rooms on the other side look out over the front lawn and flower beds. Jocelyn showed us two rooms that were currently available. Both were larger than we had expected. One of the available rooms was at the end of the hall and had windows on two sides. The other was nice, but smaller and had just one window. They both felt open and airy. No sense of being shut in or locked inside and no nursing home smell."

Taking a sip of my coffee, I asked Adele. "What do residents do all day? Spend most of the day in their rooms?"

"No, it's not like that at all," Adele resumed more cheerfully. "Residents are encouraged to be up and around. We saw the dayroom, which is open from 8:00 am to 8:00 pm. It has tall windows across one wall, and, like the rooms, it felt light, airy, and clean. There was a lot going on: crafts, cards, and groups of people talking, some sitting silently at tables or in wheelchairs. Through an archway there was a second room with a large-screen TV, several couches, and some comfortable chairs. It didn't look like home, but it looked safe and clean, and the residents all looked well cared for."

I said, "Boy, it does sound nice."

Adele continued, "Jory, I was so relieved by everything we saw and heard. I know Jack would be safe and well cared for there. It felt like a great weight was being lifted from me. I've tried my very best to keep him at home, but I just can't do it any longer."

Charlie interrupted, "Come on now, Mom, you did very well by him. All of us kids know what it took to keep him at home after the stroke."

"So, what's next?" I asked.

Charlie responded. "Well, some things have to happen before Dad can move there. Mom signed documents to release Dad's medical records for review by the Sunrise medical staff. That will probably take a couple of days. Then we need to bring him in for an evaluation to determine the level of care he will need. From that they will develop a treatment plan, which will determine the monthly costs. Mom was a little worried about the cost, but when we looked at the actual numbers, it worked out. Mom and Dad have long-term care insurance, which will help with a lot of the expenses until the resort sale closes. After that Mom won't have to worry about money any longer."

Adele continued, "How does all that sound to you, Jory?"

"Sounds like you've got all your bases covered. I can't imagine that you'll get any pushback from Theo or Raylene. They know how much you've been doing for Jack and that he's getting increasingly harder to handle. I know that none of you--or anyone really--wants to have to make these kinds of decisions, but I believe you are making the right one."

"And, Adele, if there's any way I can help at the resort, please let me be there for you. It's the least I can do when you've done so much for me over the years. After all, you gave me my first job and, on many occasions, helped Charlie and me finish it. Not to mention making it possible for me to buy the coolest mountain bike ever!"

I heard Adele's voice catch. "Thank you, Jory. That was kind of you. You were always just one of my girls." Then in a sentence that reminded me of the words Charlie used that day on the ledge, Adele continued, "When this is all settled down, I think all three of us need to have a real heart-to-heart talk, don't you?"

I felt my throat tighten and, though we were on the phone, I nodded. Finally, I just said, "I would like that."

Charlie texted that evening to let me know the phone call with Theo and Raylene had gone smoothly. She and Adele were going to go ahead with the plans to move Jack to Sunrise View.

Shortly after that, another text arrived. This time with cheerful news. She was meeting up with Aunt Rose to look at apartments the next day.

I texted back to ask if she would like to go out for dinner at El Gato, my favorite Mexican restaurant, the next night. I didn't mention it in the text, but I was very interested to hear the results of her apartment hunting with Aunt Rose the next day!

She responded with a "thumbs up."

CHAPTER 18

April 13 - 14, 2011

When I arrived at El Gato, the restaurant was already busy, and I was glad to have made a reservation. I loved this unpretentious restaurant where the food was delicious and the décor charming. The host called my name soon after I arrived, just as Charlie came in the door. Seeing her made my heart beat just a little faster. I waved to get her attention. When she saw me, her smile made my night!

I moved my hand around to the small of her back as the host led us to a booth toward the back of the restaurant. I found myself always wanting to touch her, her hand, her shoulder.... Doing so made me feel safe and connected to her. I hadn't felt like this for a very long time.

Our table was beside a large window that overlooked an outdoor fountain and seating area. At El Gato, the best tables were a perk of being a regular customer. The host handed us menus and told us that a waiter would be by to take our drink orders in just a few moments.

"Before we talk about anything else, congratulations on getting your sub certificate!" I grinned, and we high-fived across the table. From Charlie's smile, it was evident that she too was pleased.

"I called the school district to see what I needed to do to get on the sub list for the middle and high schools. They wanted me to come in for an interview. I was surprised by that. Guess they are desperate for help. I have an appointment with the District Administrator for Substitute Teachers, Daniel Tso, tomorrow. The woman I talked to said it was just a formality, but I am still really looking forward to it."

Just then the server showed up at our table with a large basket of fresh, warm tortilla chips, two kinds of salsa, and a small bowl of refried beans. "Are you ready to order your drinks?" she asked. I motioned to Charlie to order first. "I would like a mojito, please." I ordered a blood orange margarita. You really can't go wrong pairing a margarita with Mexican cuisine, and El Gato was known for the quality and variety of their flavored margaritas.

We studied and discussed the menu and, after some back and forth, decided on our orders. We caught up on one another's activities that day until the server returned with our drinks and to take our dinner orders. On my recommendation, Charlie ordered pork carnitas and I ordered chile rellenos with beans but no rice. Charlie looked across the table at me and smiled. "I see you still have that thing about rice, hmm?"

"I do," I admitted, a little embarrassed that I had not overcome my childhood dislike of rice with Mexican food. "I know it makes no sense to some, but my brain thinks rice should be reserved for Asian cuisine." I quickly changed the subject to avoid the distinct possibility that Charlie would launch off on a lengthy discourse on my idiosyncrasies. "How did your apartment hunting go?"

Charlie took a sip of her mojito. "I had forgotten how fun it was to spend time with Aunt Rose! I hope it's okay with you if I call her Aunt Rose? That's what you call her and what we always called her when I was a girl, it just seems natural to me but…"

I held up my hand in the universal signal for "Stop!" "Of course, it's fine. I like that you call her Aunt Rose and I know she likes it too. She told me so at her birthday party."

My eyes strayed to her alluring, perfectly shaped narrow lips. I watched as Charlie picked up a chip and carefully dipped it first into the hottest of the two salsas, scooped out a little of the refried beans, then lifted the loaded chip delicately into her mouth, a bit at a time. I found myself ridiculously kind of jealous of that tortilla chip.

Charlie looked at me oddly for a moment, then continued. "Well, Aunt Rose certainly knows the rental market here. She arranged for me to see apartments in five different complexes. I'd really appreciate your opinion about which, if any, of these you think I should consider." She turned to pull out a packet of papers just as the server returned with our food. One look at the steaming plates and we decided that we really should eat before we started our review of apartments. We were both suddenly starving!

The meal was even better than I remembered from previous visits. Perhaps it was the company. Charlie declared that she had now found her "go-to" Mexican restaurant, and that it was one of the best Mexican meals she'd ever eaten; a big compliment from someone who had spent the last seven years in L.A. where authentic Mexican food was a staple. I was so glad that she liked El Gato as much as I did. After dinner we changed our plans. Looking around at the number of people waiting to be seated, we decided to finish our conversation at my house. She agreed, and we made our way out of the restaurant.

Ernie welcomed us as we came through the door. I bent down to scratch him gently under his chin. When he was tired of that, he ambled over to allow Charlie to pay tribute. After Ernie had his fill of admiration from both of us, the satisfied feline trotted off toward the back of the house.

We humans moved into the kitchen and sat down at the island where Charlie had room to spread out all her brochures and notes. She'd made a wish list of what she hoped for in her new apartment. She wanted a ground floor unit with at least one bedroom, a dishwasher, laundry facilities, plus assigned and covered parking, all within her rental price range. I suggested we create a spreadsheet. Smiling gently at me, Charlie said she didn't think that would be necessary for just five apartments to consider, but we could keep that option open. My heart thumped. This is another thing I had always loved about Charlie. She could have made fun of my tendency to over-complicate things, but she never had. By way of thanking her, I leaned in and kissed her. She kissed me back in a manner that told me she wasn't really thinking about apartments. We finally pulled back to catch our breaths.

Charlie put her warm hand on my arm. "Hold that thought until we have made our decisions on the apartment." She turned her attention to the information laid out on the island. "I have to decide quickly so that I don't have to pay another month of storage and can get my things delivered as close to my move-in date as possible."

I suggested that we narrow down the list by first looking only at the apartments that met all her "must-haves." We eliminated two right off the bat. One had no parking, and the other was on the second floor. Then she considered other factors like storage space, views, square footage, amenities like a swimming pool and cable TV, and the distance to the high and middle schools. I thought that a spreadsheet would have made making the decision so much easier, but I kept my opinion to myself. After some discussion, we narrowed the choices down to two.

Glancing at the clock, we saw it was already 10:00. Charlie stood up. "I'd better get going. You have school tomorrow and I have my interview at the district."

Surprised that the time had passed by so quickly, I felt a little sad as Charlie began to gather up her belongings. "Thank you so much for dinner tonight and the help in homing in on an apartment. I really appreciate it."

"It's actually in my best interest. I am hoping to spend a lot of time there." I squeezed her hand. "Charlie, please give me a call tomorrow after your interview. I really want to know how it goes."

Charlie smiled and nodded. "You can count on it!"

We walked to the door holding hands. She kissed me goodbye, which turned into quite a bit more before she headed out into the night. I followed her out to make sure she made it to her car safely, and we shared one last goodnight kiss. Watching until after she turned out of my driveway and the Camry's taillights disappeared in the distance, I turned to go back inside. I thought about Charlie for a long time that night.

The next morning, Charlie called during my prep period to tell me about the interview she'd had with Daniel Tso at the district office. Interestingly, Camille, the high school principal, and a vice-principal from the middle school joined the meeting. The interview had gone well, and she had hit it off with all three of the administrators.

At the end of the interview, Daniel confirmed that Charlie had met the qualifications (and then some) for subbing at Mountain View and was pleased that she was interested in subbing at both the middle and high school levels. He also informed Charlie that he personally would place her on the priority sub list. This guaranteed she would be among the first to be called when a sub was needed at either school.

Charlie excitedly continued, "Daniel surprised me by asking if I would be interested in longer-term work with the district? He said the district is always looking for good candidates with a strong English and Language Arts background and mentioned the positive recommendations I received from my references. I told him that I was very interested in a full-time teaching position and was just waiting for my license to be processed before I began looking around for openings. Daniel also showed me how to check for Mountain View vacancy postings online."

To say that Charlie and I were both excited by the interview and what it might portend would be an understatement.

CHAPTER 19

April 15 - 17, 2011

In the late afternoon, Charlie called to update me on Jack's evaluation at Sunrise View. "It all went well. The Facility Doctor, Director of Nursing, Security Supervisor, as well as Jocelyn, and her assistant, Marlene Dempsey, were all waiting for us when we arrived. Jocelyn introduced everyone and explained that while the team conducted my father's assessment, we would be choosing a room and taking care of some paperwork.

"Jocelyn took us through a more comprehensive tour of the facility and the grounds. As we walked, she went over the baseline monthly fees. She told us the monthly charge would be adjusted based on the results of the evaluation now taking place and the size of the room we selected. We looked again at the two rooms that were available. Mom really liked the corner room. It was a little more expensive, but the view from the second window made it well worth it. I agreed with her completely. Dad had always loved birds and right outside of the window was a large Crepe Myrtle that seemed to be filled with finches, sparrows and chickadees might keep him calmer.

"We went back to Jocelyn's office where she gave Mom a sheaf of papers to read and sign. Some of them were straightforward, but we had questions about others. Jocelyn patiently answered every question.

"When they called us back into the evaluation meeting, I think both Mom and I were nervous. The assistant director told us that the team had completed the evaluation and pegged Dad's care level at 7 out of 10. She explained that this was a little higher than their usual intake, but it was well within the level of care they could provide. They gave Mom the evaluation report and told us that the next step for the team would be to develop an individualized treatment plan for him. She also explained that, for the first week, Sunrise asked that new residents not have any outside visitors while they adjust to the surroundings and routines. They invited us to ask any questions we had of the team or about its decisions. We only had a few questions, and the responses built our confidence that Dad would be safe and well cared-for there."

"After the evaluation, they wheeled Dad down to his room where a new bed had already been installed and made up for him. As instructed, Mom had brought a week's worth of clothing and some of his personal items, which she put away for him in the dresser, closet, and cabinets. Then everyone except Mom left, giving her some time alone with Dad to help him get settled and say goodbye. They both cried a little at what was and what might have been. Soon, though, he succumbed to the busy day and his head began to nod. The attendants helped him into bed and, by the time Mom was ready to leave, Dad was sound asleep."

"The ride home was quiet; we both believed that we had done what had been necessary and we found a sense of relief in the decision."

"You and your mom made all the right decisions," I stated with confidence.

There was a long silence before Charlie spoke again. "The entire time I was at Sunrise, I couldn't help but think how much kinder my mom was being to my father than he had been to her or me. It's really, really hard for me even to be in the same room with him, Jory."

"Your mom is a good person. If, as you believe, your father abused your mother, she would have had plenty of time to get even with him after the stroke. Instead, she consistently chose to do what was best for Jack, even when it was at her expense. Watching her kindness toward him, I don't think it's possible that she knew of, much less agreed with, any of the things

Jack did to you. Take forcing you to attend college in southern California; she never would have condoned that. First of all, it's obvious that she loves having you around. If she was going to force you to attend a college, it would much more likely be closer than WSU, not further away. Secondly, she always encouraged our friendship. Doing something as underhanded as sabotaging your application to WSU or withholding money you had earned in order to force you to attend USC is just not her. I think your father was lying."

Charlie kept silent a long time, then said, "I think you're right."

In the quiet that followed, I reflected on Adele and Charlie's hard day. I assumed Charlie was probably feeling pretty conflicted emotionally and would need some time to process everything. She would likely want to stay close to her mom for a while. But I had learned my lesson. I would not *guess* what she wanted or needed. I would talk to her and *ask* what she wanted. So, I asked.

"You know, with everything that's going on with your folks, it's easy to lose sight of what's going on with you. How are you doing?" I asked.

"This probably sounds awful, Jory, but most of the time I just feel relieved knowing I'll never have to deal with him again. But then I think about how different he was when I was a very little girl and wonder how he could have changed so much. We'll never know now. It's too late to ask him. Mostly, I want to quit thinking about him and the past. I want to focus on the present and future, *our* present and future."

"Jory, if you're not busy, would you like to come over tonight?"

Exactly why asking is better than guessing, I thought. But what I said was, "Of course! Want me to pick up some Chinese takeout? You know...the food that *should* be served with rice?"

"That sounds great. Oooh, and get us some fried shrimp too, and don't forget the fortune cookies!"

I smiled. "You're so predictable! I'll see you in a few."

I called in an order at my favorite Chinese restaurant, the Golden Dragon: wonton soup, pork chow mein, spring rolls and, of course, fried shrimp…and rice. This would be an Asian feast. Thinking about the upcoming evening, I hesitated. Tomorrow was Saturday and I really had nowhere I had to be. I threw my toothbrush and a change of clothes in a bag, just in case. After making sure that Ernie's bowls were full, I was out the door.

With my arms full of bags and boxes of Chinese food, I walked through the parking lot toward Charlie's cabin. I noticed that Adele's car was not in the lot and hoped there was not already some problem at Sunrise View.

Charlie must have been watching for me because the door swung open the moment I stepped onto the porch. "Wow, being here sure brings back a lot of memories." I had cleaned this very cabin more times than I could count. I took a professional look around to see if it still looked inviting, clean, and well maintained.

"The place looks good," I began. Before I could add another word, Charlie practically grabbed the bags out of my hands. "I'm famished. Let's eat!"

We set the various boxes out on the table and began to fill our plates. We ate without talking. It was a comfortable silence, and we were both very happy. After dinner, we cleared our plates and stored the leftovers in the refrigerator. Then, we read our fortunes from the cookies. Charlie's said, "You make friends easily." Mine predicted, "Your wish will come true." I thought Charlie's was accurate and hoped that mine would come true.

I looked into Charlie's eyes, trying to read her mind, then asked, "It's a warm evening. Want to take a walk down to the lake…maybe get a canoe?"

"No!" And with that, she reached out to me and pulled me in close, her soft lips crashing into mine. I deepened the kiss and our kisses turned hungry. I ran my tongue along her lower lip requesting her to allow me entrance and she complied. She tasted wonderful, like mint tea. That combined with her signature scent of lime and coconut made conscious thought almost impossible. My passion for Charlie, repressed for so long, ignited. My dream of so many years was right in front of me, and I knew exactly where I wanted this to lead. "Charlie, do you want to?... Are you ready to?... Do you think it's too?..." Saving me from further babbling, she reached down, took my hand, and led me to her bedroom. So much for wanting to go slow.

That night was more than I could ever have dreamed. I thought our first time together would be gentle and tentative. Charlie had other ideas. We practically ripped each other's clothes off as we fell onto the bed. Touching her, skin to skin, was so erotic that I thought for a moment I might pass out. Charlie's soft moans and eager touch showed me she was experiencing feelings every bit as intense as mine.

Much later that night, my heart somehow felt larger than it had before. We fell asleep pressed closely together. It was hard to tell where one began and the other ended, which foot or arm belonged to whom. We clung to one another through the night.

The early morning sun on my face awakened me. Charlie was still asleep next to me, her face soft and sunlit. I was so happy to be there with her, my emotions overwhelmed me. Tears stung my eyes and my breath caught for just a second. We had waited so long. Now, there was a real chance for the "forever" we had promised one another as girls.

I quietly slipped out of bed, borrowed the robe hanging on the back of the door and padded to the kitchen to make coffee. I rustled around until I found what I needed to get the coffeemaker started. While I waited for it to brew, I enjoyed.... well, everything. Jory's scent on the warm robe, the sun coming up over the mountain, the aroma of the brewing coffee, the cozy little cabin that Charlie had somehow made her own. A feeling of euphoria washed over me. I felt wonderful!

In the middle of my reverie, the coffee was ready. Even in high school, Charlie loved coffee first thing in the morning. I poured two mugs full and made my way back to the little bedroom. I set our hot cups on the nightstand and gently welcome her into wakefulness with a peck on her cheek.

One of Charlie's most endearing traits is that she always wakes up with a smile on her face. As I saw that smile begin to form, I couldn't for my life have kept from leaning down and fully kissing her. Her beautiful hazel eyes met mine and her smile broadened. "Where is that coffee I smell?" she croaked. Okay...not really a sexy morning greeting, but I thought it was adorable.

After a sip or two of her coffee, she looked up at me. "I know we have been apart for a long time, Jory, but I never stopped thinking of you or wanting to be with you. I love you so much, Jory. I always have and I always will. Last night was everything I have dreamed of for so long."

Now *that* was a sexy, good morning greeting!

As I started to speak, Charlie put her finger on my lips. "No, wait. I hurt you so much and for so long, Jory. I will never forgive my father for what he did, and I can't forgive myself for not standing up to him. It cost us years. I don't want you to feel like you have to say anything back to me now. But, when you *are* ready, I'll be waiting for you, no matter how long it takes."

I didn't need any time. "Charlie, we were just kids when all that ugliness happened. You and I have made mistakes, it's true, but it was mostly because we didn't know any better. The true fault lies squarely on Jack's shoulders, he knew exactly what he was doing. It wasn't you or me that cost us those years."

I hurried to explain before Charlie could stop me. "There never has been anyone else but you for me either. But I do understand that you don't want me to say those three big words back to you right away. You want me to think about it for a while. Well, I have been thinking about it for the past seven years. Even so, I will honor your request to wait a bit. Hmmm, it's 8:30 am now, how about if I wait until 9:00? Will that be okay?"

Charlie pulled me down and I fell into her in every way. At 9:00 Charlie and I were otherwise engaged. This time we enjoyed the gentle lovemaking we had not managed the night before. I was able to work those three little words in at an appropriate moment.

Later, relaxing in the early morning sunlight, I sat part way up, resting my chin in my hand. "Charlie, I want you to know this. I don't just love you. I love you more than anything in the world. I think I have since the 2nd grade and expect I always will. I've had years to think about how I feel about you and I've never been so sure of anything in my life!" We both laughed out loud with the sheer joy of it.

We talked, we made love, and we didn't eat breakfast/lunch until after 1:00. Thank goodness for leftover Chinese. After that, I had to go back home to take care of Ernie. Charlie wanted to check in with Adele to see if she was still feeling okay about Jack's move to Sunrise View. The two of them also needed to work out how Charlie would juggle substitute teaching with her responsibilities at the resort.

We agreed that Charlie would come by my place later in the afternoon and we would drive by the two apartments she was considering. After that we'd grab dinner and maybe watch another movie. Since Charlie had to work at the resort on Sunday and I had papers to grade and errands to run, our weekend together would be a short one.

As I neared my front door, I heard Ernie's welcoming "meow." I could tell he had missed me, because he didn't leave my side for the next hour. I told him about everything that had happened between Charlie and me. Ernie liked Charlie.

A couple of hours later, I opened the door to welcome her in. The kiss that ensued left me breathless. We both knew that if we wanted to see the apartments today, we needed to leave now!

We clocked the distance from each apartment to the middle and high schools, downtown, good restaurants and other important services. As we drove, I could not stop touching Charlie.

My hand was resting on her thigh. It took stern mental discipline not to allow that wayward hand to creep higher. Charlie seemed to suffer from the same malady. She had her hand around the back of my neck, gently massaging the taut muscles there.

After comparing the two apartments, we agreed that the Village Green apartment came out ahead on all counts. It was located closer to work and services, but not so close to down-town that noise and traffic would be a problem. Two other elements factored in our decision. At Village Green, a stacked, space-saving washer and dryer were provided in each apartment and, in the one Charlie had decided to apply for, the large living room window framed a Mountain Ash tree and small stream just outside of her window. Once her decision was made, Charlie completed the rental application and we stopped by the office to turn it in along with the application fee.

On the way home, we stopped at Dave's Diner, known for the best burgers in town. It's been in the same location for over 20 years. "Dave" (whose real name is Roy) was 28 when he opened the diner in 1990. He thought it would appeal to the high school crowd. It did that, but once word got around about just how good the food was, it began to draw people of all ages. Dave kept the 12 tables and eight seat counter spotlessly clean and in mint condition. We'd loved Dave's back in the day. Charlie looked up in surprise after taking a few minutes to study the menu. "Has this menu changed at all? I swear these are the exact same burgers we used to get here when we were in middle and high school."

"They still taste just as good too," I assured her.

After we had placed our order, I asked, "Did you and Adele work out your teaching and resort work schedules?"

"I explained to Mom that I needed to get as many sub jobs as possible for two reasons. One, I need the money, and two, I want the administrators and teachers to have a chance to get to know me. There are only seven weeks left in the school year. I think having people get to know me a little and see my teaching style will give me an advantage when I apply for a full-time teaching position. Mom was very understanding about me needing to leave my job at the resort a few days earlier than planned. I was only supposed to work there until the sale closed, anyway."

Charlie continued, "Ramona, one of the housekeepers, has a sister who's looking for work. Mom is considering hiring her. If she does, I would be able to start subbing right away. Mom again offered to help me financially until I got settled. But rent and everything else is so much less expensive here, I think I can make it until I get my first paycheck. If not, then I can take her up on her offer."

When the burgers arrived, Charlie took her first bite and mumbled through a full mouth, "This burger is fantastic."

Pleased that she liked her burger, I added, "Wait until you try the chocolate milkshake, I ordered for us to share for dessert."

I reached over and wiped a spot of ketchup from the corner of Charlie's lips. The connection I felt when my fingers contacted her lips made me doubt whether we would be seeing a movie tonight after all. Turned out, I was right.

Charlie left early Sunday morning to work her shift at the resort. As I came back inside after seeing her off, the house felt empty. I had been totally content to live alone for the past three years, but that changed almost overnight. I am not proud to admit that I moped around for a while wishing Charlie could have stayed. I gave myself a firm lecture about not acting like a baby and made myself get busy with housekeeping, laundry, and grocery shopping. Once those chores were finished, I settled in to grade lab reports so that I could return them to students on Monday. Oh, and I also took a short, well-deserved nap...on "her side" of the bed.

CHAPTER 20

April 19 - April 25, 2011

Monday Charlie worked at the resort and, that evening, began packing some of her things for the move to her new apartment. She'd also received her first subbing assignment which was set for the following day. On Tuesday Charlie went back to school. This time as a brand-new substitute teacher at MVHS. She would be covering 3 days of 12th grade American Literature and 10th grade AP English classes while the regular teacher was out on personal leave. She felt empathy for the teacher on leave and hoped it wasn't a family emergency like the stroke that had pulled her from the classroom.

When the lunch bell sounded, I walked down to the room where Charlie was subbing. I loved seeing her in that classroom. Grown-up Charlie looked so darned cute sitting in the big chair behind the teacher's desk. It was like a little peek into the future. Looking up, she spotted me. I could tell by the big smile on her face that she was having a good day. She grabbed her lunch sack from a drawer in the desk and we walked down to the faculty lunchroom where I introduced her around. A couple of the teachers remembered her from when she was a student at MVHS and two more teachers remembered her from when we were all in school together, though neither were in our same year. In a matter of minutes, she was chatting amiably with everyone. She had always made friends so easily and you could see it happening again. People were just naturally drawn to her. I was so proud!

After school Charlie checked her email and found that her rental application had been approved. She decided that she'd schedule her move-in date for the coming Friday, the 22nd. She was hoping the moving company could deliver her car and household goods from L.A. on Saturday. I planned to help her move in and get settled on Saturday and Sunday. The only hang-up was that the moving company had called Charlie back and let her know that it was unlikely that they could put a crew together to move her load to Mountain View by Saturday. But they would do their best.

After school on Thursday, we went together to the Village Green's rental office to pick up the keys to Charlie's new apartment and drop off the first and last month's rent. The on-site manager was very nice in allowing us to go in and look around the day before the occupancy date. Charlie pronounced this a reconnaissance mission, explaining that she needed to look around to see what she's going to need to buy. As we checked out each room, Charlie's list grew longer. Even though it was likely that some of the things she was now putting on her to-buy list would be in the boxes on their way up from her L.A. storage unit, she thought it better to get them on her list now while she was thinking of them and cross them off later if they turned up in the truck. We took several measurements of walls, and floors for rugs and furniture placement.

It really was a nice apartment, with good light and space. The open kitchen and living room design made the rooms seem larger than they were. The gas fireplace would be great in the cold Idaho winter, and the idyllic view from the large front window would be beautiful in every season. There was an area in the kitchen that would be perfect for a small table and 4 chairs.

The bath was not huge, but not too small either. Everything looked relatively new and very clean. It would do just fine.

The bedroom felt a little tight, but the large walk-in closet made up for it. There was just enough room for the queen-size bed and nightstands to fit. Charlie thought that the walk-in closet would easily hold all her clothes with room to spare. If she could fit her dresser in the closet, it would make the room feel more spacious. We'd have to wait for the furniture to be delivered to tell for sure.

Charlie wanted to have dinner with her mother at the resort and sleep in her little cabin one more night before leaving for the last time on Friday. She was feeling a little sentimental at spending her last night there. In just a few days the Clear Springs Lake Resort would no longer part of her world. I hugged Charlie close, kissed her gently, and we parted ways for the evening.

Charlie wasn't scheduled to work on Friday. She planned to use the day to pack up her belongings from the cabin and use Jack's SUV to take them to the apartment. If she could get that much transferred to the apartment, she'd have a head start on the move. By the time I arrived at the apartment after school on Friday, Charlie had already put everything from the cabin into the cabinets and closets in her new place. Charlie called to let her mom know that she had moved out of the cabin, so it was available for the housekeepers to give it a deep cleaning. New guests were already scheduled to arrive on Sunday.

The new bed arrived late that afternoon and was set up by the delivery guys. I was secretly glad that the bed she and Liam slept in wasn't one of the pieces of furniture Charlie was bringing up from L.A. I really didn't want to sleep in the bed they had shared but I would have been willing to swap it for the one in my guest room. Her foresight had rendered the need for that uncomfortable conversation unnecessary. I brought over a set of sheets, a couple of blankets and some pillows to use until she could get her own set from the boxes on their way up from L.A.

There was also good news from the moving company. They'd been able to scrape together a moving crew on short notice so they could deliver her car, furniture, and household goods on Saturday morning after all. Things were looking bright.

Saturday's big move-in went smoothly. The truck from L.A. arrived just before 9:00 am and the movers began unloading everything, with no time wasted. All the boxes had been labeled for the rooms where they belonged, but the movers didn't seem to care when Charlie changed her mind several times. They just placed the furniture wherever she pointed. They finished in less than an hour. There hadn't really been that much to move.

Once the movers had departed, Charlie and I went to work unpacking and putting everything away. By the end of the day, we had her apartment in order. Even the boxes had been broken down and taken to the recycling area at the side of the complex. It was fun to walk from room to room to see how Charlie had transformed the bare rooms into inviting living spaces and already created a home. We were finished, flagging, and famished.

Charlie was dead set on us spending the first night together in her new apartment. I had brought coffee and rolls for breakfast the next morning and we decided on a Margherita pizza and Greek salad from Roberto's Pizzeria for dinner. We called in an order for delivery that would take about 45 minutes. That gave us time to walk down to the parking area to see Charlie's newly delivered Miata.

The Miata was a hot looking little sportscar, made more so by its candy apple red paint job. It totally looked like something Charlie would drive. I could see why she loved it. I was torn between thinking how much fun we could have in it this summer and my concern for how safe it would be in our snowy Idaho winters. Well, winter was a long way off and a lot of fun could be had between now and then. I oohed and aahed over the little roadster for several minutes before we headed back into the apartment for dinner.

The pizza arrived shortly after we got back. We made short work of it. After dinner we put some gas in the SUV and drove back to the resort to drop it off. The SUV was one of the assets listed in the sales contract and so would belong to the Cordovas at the end of the day tomorrow although they had agreed Charlie and her mom could use it during whenever they needed it during the one-month transition period. We stopped to catch up with Adele for just a moment before heading back to Charlie's apartment at the Village Greens.

When I turned around after closing and locking the front door, she took my hands and, walking backwards, led me toward the bedroom to, as Charlie put it, "test out the new bed." We gave it a thorough testing.

Lying in bed on Sunday morning, I reflected on the most sensual night of my life. I was idly caressing Charlie's hip and imagining our next 10 years together, when a question popped into my mind.

"Charlie?"

"Hmm?" she answered, her eyes still closed.

"You know the first day you subbed at MVHS and we had lunch with the other teachers at school?"

'Yes. But please don't stop doing what you're doing."

"I won't. But I wasn't sure how to describe our relationship when I introduced you."

"You weren't? Silly Jory. I'm your girlfriend."

"That's what I thought, but I just wanted to make sure."

"Jory, I know it's hard for you to believe that people in your life won't leave you," she said sitting up on her elbows and looking me in the eyes. "And yes, we did get separated, but it was by force, not by choice. No one will ever again be in a position to force us apart. For me, this is forever, and I plan to spend every day of the rest of my life proving that to you."

With those words, the very last little niggling worry that Charlie was not "all in" simply blew away like fine dust before a gentle wind.

"I love you, you know, Charlie."

"Jory, I think you showed that to me last night and again this morning, don't you?"

"Well, I love this new bed too."

"So do I," Charlie smiled, and we turned our attention to other matters.

And so, the best, most fun, most languorous day of my life

glided by.

CHAPTER 21

April 26 - 27, 2011

April 26th was an important day for Adele. She signed the final papers turning ownership of the Clear Springs Lake Resort over to the new owners, Ron and Cathy Cordova. Adele had invited Charlie and me to celebrate the sale over dinner that night at the River House. Adele surprised me by inviting my mom, too. The River House is the best restaurant in Mountain View, and certainly the most expensive. I was pleased to have been invited along and tickled that my mother was included.

Charlie thought that Adele might have developed a case of seller's remorse, but it was just the opposite. Adele was relieved, almost giddy. She explained, "I feel so free, even lighthearted. I loved the resort, but it's time for younger people to take over with new plans and ideas. Ron and Cathy are a delightful couple, and it was such fun to see them so excited. That's exactly the way Jack and I felt when we bought it. The only sadness I feel is that Jack has missed out on so much, and not just since his stroke. Actually, things changed a long time before that."

Now was not the time, but I know that Charlie and I both wanted to ask Adele a lot more about what "Jack missed out on so much" and why and when "things changed." Adele and Tess exchanged a knowing glance, and then, as if reading our minds, Adele added, "I know we need to talk about Jack and what happened over the last 10 years, but perhaps not tonight?"

We readily agreed. Tonight, was for celebrating.

The four of us had a great time. Sharing two bottles of very good and very expensive champagne definitely added to the gaiety. We laughed over some of the things that had occurred at the resort over the years and reminisced about our most and least favorite guests. We remembered Aunt Rose's antics with the troublesome-twosome and laughed a lot. It was a delightful dinner.

As the evening wore down, Adele had one last announcement she wanted to make. "Charlie, you have stood by me unwaveringly over the last seven months, giving up your apartment, your job, and even your friends in L.A."

I was grateful she didn't mention Liam.

Adele reached into her pocket and pulled out a small box. "I wanted to show you how much I appreciate all that you've done for me. But you wouldn't take any money, so..." She handed the neatly wrapped package to Charlie. Charlie unwrapped the box to reveal a set of car keys. Charlie's face displayed puzzlement, but her eyes glistened as she looked up to meet her mother's eyes.

Adele smiled lovingly at Charlie. "That Miata of yours is great for cruising around in the summer, but for winter-time driving around here you're going to need something that can stand up to our weather. When you get back to your apartment, there's a new Honda CR-V 4WD waiting for you."

For a moment all three of us were stunned speechless by Adele's gift. Charlie jumped out of her chair and ran around the table to thank her mom with a mammoth hug, while my mother and I smiled hugely at the generous and well-deserved gift. I couldn't hear what she whispered into her mother's ear, but I could see by Adele's face she was touched and very, very pleased.

When things calmed down a bit, Adele added a few details. She had arranged for Charlie to have 72 hours to decide if the CR-V Adele had selected was right for her. Adele encouraged her to go down to the dealer and look around to see if there was a different make, model or even color she would rather have.

Then Adele called for dessert. We all split a huge piece of flourless chocolate cake topped with vanilla ice cream. It was rich and decadent, and we loved every bite.

It was a wonderful evening. It was also a demonstration of how well Adele knew her daughter. After getting the first look at her new SUV when we returned to the apartment, Charlie declared that she loved everything about it, including its metallic bright red color. She immediately called her mother to thank her again and tell her she was keeping the CR-V she'd picked out. I was relieved to know that she'd be driving a car better suited for winter conditions. But I was also glad Charlie wouldn't need to trade in the Miata. I was looking forward to riding around in that cute little thing this summer.

Charlie invited me to dinner at her apartment the next evening for what would be Charlie's first meal, cooked from scratch, in her new home. It was an experience. She had decided she would make lasagna and a green salad. We laughed repeatedly as we tried to remember where we'd put the sage, oregano, and garlic powder, where the colander had been stashed, where the jar opener might be found, and why we'd put the spatula in the knife drawer. It was as much a scavenger hunt as dinner preparation. Despite the difficulties, the lasagna was quite tasty, and the tossed salad of fresh baby greens made the perfect side dish. We never did find the aluminum foil.

CHAPTER 22

May 2 - May 5, 2011

Over the next few weeks things seemed to fall into place almost effortlessly. Perhaps the universe had just decided to be kind. Charlie was called in to sub nearly every day. We spent most nights together at either her house or mine and our relationship continued to deepen.

Charlie invited me to dinner at her place to talk about the teacher vacancy notices the district had posted online the day before. There were two full-time English positions open. One was at the high school teaching literature, writing and journalism to 10th and 12th grade students. The other was at the middle school teaching English to 7th and 8th graders. The expected opening for a summer session English teacher was also posted. That one started in mid-June and ran for 6 weeks.

Charlie was beginning to be concerned at how long it was taking the Idaho Department of Education to approve her license. I didn't tell Charlie, but I was getting a little worried too. A lot rested on Charlie getting a decent-paying, full-time job with benefits. As soon as her license was issued, she would qualify for all three positions. Both the full-time and summer school positions paid much more than substituting, provided paid health insurance coverage and offered a 401(k)-retirement program. These were important considerations for Charlie. Of course, I would support whatever decision she made but I would love it if we could teach at the same school.

The evening was so temperate that we decided to cook outdoors. It was a reprise of the meal we shared on our first date and made me reflect again on how much I enjoyed having Charlie back in my life. As we finished dinner, I looked over at her. I loved it when she wore her hair down as she did this night. Her lips were the perfect shape. I loved the spot where her neck met her shoulders. I wanted to....

Charlie caught me staring at her and her twinkling eyes told me that she knew exactly where my thoughts had strayed. Her next words confirmed it. "Not so fast, Romeo. First, we talk; then we canoodle."

We grabbed our icy glasses of Sauvignon Blanc and I (only slightly dejected) followed her from the kitchen into the living room to talk about her career decisions.

We settled on Charlie's comfortable teal blue couch as she began, "Okay. Here is what I have been thinking about. I decided that what I really want is the position at the high school. My degree is in literature, but I've also taught writing and journalism, so I have the requisite experience and I love those subjects. I would probably be happy teaching at the middle school, but I think I'd enjoy the high school age group more.

"On the other hand, while I want the high school position most, right now my most important consideration is getting *any* job that has good pay and benefits, period. There's no telling when the next English position will be open at either school. I'm thinking that applying for both positions might be a good idea. But if I apply for both jobs, do you think it would look like I just want any old job and don't care which one I get? That could open the door to questions about my commitment. That's a message I don't want to send. What do you think, Jory?"

"You're saying that your first priority is getting a full-time job with benefits, and your second priority is getting the assignment you like best. Whichever way it goes, I know you'll give your best effort every day," I said with confidence.

"Exactly," Charlie concurred.

"So that answers your question, doesn't it?"

"Yes, it does. Thanks for helping me see everything so clearly.

I'll apply for both and if they ask me in the interview about my commitment to either position, I will say exactly what you just said."

"Okay," I continued. "Now let's talk about summer school. Why do you want to apply to teach summer school?"

"I need the money," she admitted a bit sheepishly. "I used up most of my savings staying up here for six months without a job. Going back and forth to L.A., moving, and renting the apartment cost me quite a bit too. Subbing brought in some money, but it wasn't that much better than minimum wage. I really can't afford to go another three months without at least some income."

"Then teaching at the summer session seems to be something you *need* to do. Plus, it can be a lot of fun. It's a lot more relaxed than the regular school year. The classes are smaller, and you can even hold some of your lessons outdoors if you want to," I explained, as I took a sip of my wine.

"But if I'm working for those six weeks, what will you do?"

I smiled to myself thinking of all the summers I had spent without Charlie, or anyone really, over the past seven years. I can't say I was unhappy in those years, but I knew I would be so much happier this year now that Charlie was here with me. Just to hear her ask that question pleased me at a deep level. She was making plans based on us. It made our relationship seem more substantial, and firm. I didn't say any of that out loud.

What I did say was, "I've been wanting to take the Ethnobotany summer class offered at Clearwater Community College. It runs the same six weeks as the high school summer session. For the first six weeks of our summer vacation, you can teach, and I'll take my class. After that, we can go somewhere on our first ever vacation together. That will give us time to enjoy summer here too. It'll be perfect! We have lots of time to plan a terrific vacation trip. We just need to decide where we want to go."

Charlie snuggled a little closer to me and kissed me just below my ear in that special spot that always gave me goose bumps. I smiled down at her. "We'll have a great summer," I murmured as I became increasingly distracted. I always enjoyed the plotting and planning of any trip or project almost as much as the activity itself. But it could wait for a bit.

I hadn't told Charlie, but I suspected that she had a lock on the summer school position. A few days after Charlie's interview with the district regarding substitute teaching, Camille, the MVHS principal, had asked me if I thought Charlie might be interested in teaching over the summer. The teacher who had been teaching English for the past several years was retiring and all the other high school English teachers already had summer plans. I assured Camille that Charlie would be very interested in the job. I was pretty sure that Camille was just waiting for Charlie's teaching license to come through before approaching Charlie directly.

Charlie's Idaho Professional Teaching License finally arrived in the mail three days after my conversation with Camille. Charlie could now apply for all three positions. She took her time getting them just right, then submitted all three at once. I mentioned to Camille that Charlie had applied for the three English positions. Now she had to wait.

There was also good news for Adele. She and Aunt Rose had found a condo that Adele really liked, and she'd made an offer on it. She promised to get Aunt Rose to schedule another showing with Charlie and me to get our opinions too. To my surprise, Adele had again invited my mom to come along. It looked like they were developing a friendship of their own. I loved the idea of that. We scheduled the showing for the following Saturday, May 7.

Adele, Mom, Aunt Rose, Charlie, and I all went to lunch together on Saturday before going to see the condo. Adele chose a sushi bar where the chef's knife-wielding skills entertained and amazed us. At first, we each chose our own lunches but, being women, once the servers delivered the meals, everyone shared with everyone else, so that when the trading was done it looked as if we all had ordered sampler plates. All of us agreed that we liked the California Rolls best. Tiny cups of warm sake made the lunch even better. Then, we set off to see the condo.

On top of a hill overlooking the river, the condominium complex stood out in stark relief against the sky. It reminded me of a military outpost strategically positioned to guard the river. It was majestic and a little imposing, modern to the point of austerity. Sort of conflicting styles. Charlie and I made eye contact and silently agreed that so far, we were not impressed.

We walked over to the large, double doors and Aunt Rose keyed in her realtor code. The click of the doors unlocking was all the invitation we needed to enter. Our opinion of the condo began to change the moment we moved into the spacious, well-designed lobby. To the right of us was the elevator. We waited without talking, stepped in when the doors whooshed open, and Aunt Rose pressed the button for the 5th floor. At the 5th floor, Aunt Rose directed us to the door of 5A.

Aunt Rose again used her realtor code to open the large bronze-colored front door and ushered us into the condo. She explained that this had been the model-unit when the condo complex was built three years before. As we entered into the main living area through a small foyer, we were awestruck. The condo was beautiful! It was furnished with high-end appliances, fixtures, and window coverings. Custom flooring was installed throughout. Everything about it said quality and elegance. Floor-to-ceiling windows in the living room and primary bedroom faced out onto the river and brought the beautiful outdoors right into the rooms. The view was striking, and the surprisingly large balcony was a bonus. According to Aunt Rose, the seller was a marine salvage consultant who had dreamed of spending his downtime in Mountain View. However, the realities of his hectic schedule meant he was only infrequently able to spend time here. As his business showed no signs of slowing down, he was now reluctantly selling the home he was seldom able to enjoy.

We talked a little about the look of the exterior. Adele, Mom, and Aunt Rose all said they liked it, while Charlie and I didn't really care for it. However, we *all* loved the interior design. Mom and Adele huddled here and there exchanging observations and ideas about how the condo could be furnished. We all agreed that the place was perfect for Adele, the exterior notwithstanding. There were now five people with their fingers crossed, hoping that Adele's offer would be accepted.

On our way home, Charlie and I talked about how different Adele's life would be after she no longer had the responsibilities of the resort. Its sale ensured that she would be financially secure for life. We wondered aloud what she might do with newfound freedom. Maybe she would find something else she loved to do. Maybe she would finally be able to indulge in the travelling she had always dreamt of.

Charlie smiled as she recalled that, when she was growing up, her mom would send off for travel brochures, at first by mail and later via the internet. When the brochures arrived, Adele and all three kids would spend a fun afternoon looking through them, daydreaming about the trips they would take and the sights they would see.

We all resolved that we'd encourage Adele to step out and do some travelling now that she was no longer tied down by the 24/7 business of running Clear Springs Lake Resort. We dreamed a little ourselves about places we wanted to see and things we wanted to do. Maybe the three of us could take a short trip to rekindle Adele's wanderlust. Considering how well Adele and Mom got along, maybe we could make it a foursome.

CHAPTER 23

May 14, 2011

The next Saturday Adele invited us to visit her at the lodge to share a glass or two of wine. It was just five days after Adele's offer on the condo had been accepted. There had been some back-and-forth bargaining, but both parties had given a little to come to an agreement. She was thrilled with her purchase, and we expected to spend the evening talking about her new place. We didn't know it at the time, but we had not been invited over to talk about the future. Adele had invited us over to talk about the past.

Adele brought out a bottle of chilled Pinot Gris. She poured three glasses and we toasted to Adele's new home. Then we chatted about closing dates and moving arrangements. Charlie, now the most knowledgeable among us since her recent experience moving her things from L.A., volunteered to check out local moving companies and come back to Adele with a recommendation. The two of us volunteered to help Adele pack and move into the condo and got the dates onto our calendars.

As the conversation floated along lightly, Adele's thoughts seemed to drift. Eventually the conversation flagged. Finally, she firmly nodded her head once, as if she had made a difficult decision. "I'll be right back," she said and got up and went into the kitchen.

She returned with a second bottle of wine and topped off our glasses, even though neither the first bottle nor our glasses were yet empty. She squared her shoulders and turned to Charlie. "I've wanted to talk to you about something for a long time. I've learned the hard way just how damaging secrets can be. Not just for the person whose secret it is, but also for anyone who knows the secret and keeps it. Over the past 10 years, I've been keeping some of Jack's secrets. I thought by keeping them to myself, I would be protecting you. Instead, I think now, it may have enabled some awful things to happen."

Confused that Adele would invite me into what appeared to be a very personal and intimate conversation between a mother and daughter, I thought I should excuse myself. I started to my feet, but Adele waved me back down.

"No, Jory. You're part of this through no fault of your own. If you're willing, I'd like you stay." I glanced over at Charlie. Her uncertain expression mirrored my feelings. She nodded for me to stay.

Adele stared at the window, spoke softly but strongly, "I'll start from the beginning. When I met Jack, he was so handsome. His dark hair and beautiful smile first drew me to him. As I got to know him better, I saw other traits I admired. He was fun and laughed easily. He was thoughtful and hard working. We dated for over a year before I agreed to marry him. We had so many dreams. We wanted to work for ourselves rather than for others. We saved for that day, though with three kids it was slow going.

"That changed when my parents passed away. They left me a very generous inheritance. Looking back on it now, they may have seen something in Jack that I missed because in addition to the inheritance, they also left me a letter, asking that whatever we bought with the inheritance be kept in my name only.

"Jack and I thought a lot about what we might do with the money. We decided to use it to make our dream of working for ourselves come true. There were so many opportunities out there and we looked at a lot of them. None seemed exactly right. Then a little more than a year after my parents died, we found exactly what we had been looking for. I remember talking about its night after night. Working all the numbers on envelopes and legal pads," she stopped and smiled wistfully. "Finally, we decided to take the chance. We used my inheritance to buy the

Clear Springs Lake Resort and jumped in with both feet. Jack was not happy about putting the resort in my name alone, but I wanted to honor my parents' request, and eventually he agreed.

"The first few years at the resort were a lot of hard work but we were happy. We put every cent we earned back into improving the resort. One day, the State Forestry Department approached us with a proposition. If we would open the west end of the lake to the public, they would take over maintenance of the lake and provide us with a substantial cash payment. The cash pay-out and reduced costs in lake maintenance allowed us to breath freely for the first time since we bought the resort. We were able to hire some staff, update the lodge and cabins, and even add some amenities. Those improvements drew more guests and increased our income. The resort began to be mentioned positively in regional travel magazines.

"Eventually, we were contacted by *Resort America*, the largest travel magazine in the US. They wanted to do a spread on Clear Springs. Of course, we agreed. A writer and photographer stayed at the resort for three days researching the story and taking pictures. Four months later the article came out. It was four pages including some stunning photographs. It was the best publicity we'd ever received. It turned the corner for us. Reservations poured in and that bump has continued to this day. But there was one big problem. I had no idea the writer had found that the resort was in my name, nor that he would focus part of the article on the woman-owned aspect.

"Up to that time everyone just assumed Jack was a co-owner and he was in every way except on that damned deed. Jack was a proud man and very aware and protective of his standing in the community. When he saw the article, he was livid, and he blamed me. He accused me of intentionally belittling him in front of the whole town. No matter how many times I told him that I had no idea how the writer found out about the deed or that he was intending to highlight my ownership in the story,

Jack didn't believe me. He came back over and over again accusing me of embarrassing him in front of everyone we knew.

"Unfortunately, a lot of people in Mountain View thought the whole thing was hilarious and gave him a hard time about it, even presenting him with an "Employee of the Month" award one night at a Chamber of Commerce meeting. The more people saw it bothered him, the more they ribbed him about it. There was nothing I could do, and Jack wouldn't let it go. It changed everything between us."

I noticed Charlie sit up straighter at Adele's last words. I thought I knew why. Charlie had told me that on the day Jack forced her to stop seeing me, her father had said that going to the prom together had embarrassed him in front of his friends. Those were the exact words Charlie told me he had used!

Before I could say anything, Adele had moved on. "Jack believed I was lying to him about the article. He began to mistrust me in other aspects of our relationship as well. He started asking me where I had been and who I talked to. I noticed he watched me closely whenever he saw me talking to our male guests. I tried to reassure him, but as time went on, he seemed to get worse rather than better.

One night I had it out with him. I told him I was not his property, and he could not dictate to me, telling me where I could go or who I could see. My words triggered something in him. Before I knew what was happening, he slapped me hard enough to knock me down. We were both horrified. He ran to pick me up and apologized over and over. He said he didn't know what he was thinking. He begged me for a second chance. He swore to me it would never, ever happen again."

Clearly distressed, Charlie rose out of her seat. "Oh, my God, Mom! What did you do?"

"Looking back on it, I made a mistake I should have ended our marriage right then, but I had you three kids and everything we had was tied up in the resort. I couldn't run it by myself and, with my parents gone, I had no one to turn to. I did what so many abused women initially do, I gave him a second chance believing him when he said it was an aberration and would never happen again.

"And things did get better for a short time. But before too long he was back to making accusations. Our relationship fell into shambles. At least, he kept his word about not hitting me again. For a while, anyway."

I looked at Charlie. She was ashen colored, her head in her hands. Adele was looking at the ground, her years of silence seeming to compel her to finish relaying what she had held inside for so long.

"About the time you entered high school, Jack began to complain about how much time the two of you spent together. I thought it was just talk, but the night of the Junior Prom we had another terrible fight. This time it was over you two going to the prom together. I tried to explain to him that a lot of girls went together and that it didn't have to mean more than that. Though honestly, in my heart of hearts, I felt that it likely did.

I heard Charlie groan. My stomach was in knots. Going to the prom together seems to have been the catalyst for so much.

Still, Adele continued, "He wanted me to forbid you to go. When I told him that I wouldn't stop you, he hit me again. This time with his fist. Hard. His ring cut my lip and cheek and left a large bruise under my eye. Just like the time before, he rushed to apologize and promised it would never happen again. He begged me to forgive him. I had already given him one chance, and I bitterly regretted it. I wouldn't give him another."

Charlie interrupted, "Oh Mom! I thought he might have hurt you that night. I heard you and Dad arguing and I thought it sounded like he hit you. By the time I had enough courage to go back into the living room, you were gone, and he told me to 'get out!' He was so angry that I was afraid to talk to him at all. I just ran out as he told me to. I'm sorry, Mom. I should never have left you there with him!" Charlie was crying now.

Adele stood up, grabbed a tissue, and walked across the room to sit next to Charlie. She put her arm around Charlie, kissed the top of her head, and pressed the tissue into Charlie's palm. Then in a gentle voice said, "Honey, *none* of this was *your* fault. You were just a *girl*. Your father and I were the *adults*. *We* let *you down*, not the other way around."

I thought to myself that Charlie had been right about so much! So much damage had been caused by this man who put his imagined standing in the community above all else. What a fool to have thrown away the love of these two wonderful women.

Adele took a breath and a sip of her wine and offered "I'm sure this is as difficult for you to hear as it is for me to tell. This isn't all of what I want to share with you tonight, but how about we take a little break?"

I, too, thought we needed a break and suggested, "It's not quite dark yet, why don't we take a walk down to the lake?" Adele and Charlie nodded, seeming grateful for a distraction and some fresh air.

The three of us walked down to the dock with little said. We sat and watched the stars come out over the water. I thought about how troubled we three felt compared to the seemingly carefree guests who were gathered around the nightly resort hosted campfire. It seemed impossible that Adele's story had not affected everyone at the lodge, but the guests continued to laugh and sing and enjoy themselves, untouched by the events in Adele and Charlie's lives.

After a while, Adele said, "It's dark. Do you think we should go back?" Charlie and I mumbled agreements and sooner than I wished, we found ourselves back at the lodge. We sat in the same seats we had occupied earlier. I suggested we switch to water and brought everyone a full glass.

Adele looked straight into Charlie's eyes and picked up from where we had left off in the same sad voice she had used earlier.

"I need to finish this." Charlie met her stare and nodded.

Adele began, "After Jack hit me the second time, I knew I needed to get some professional help. I wasn't sure who to turn to until I thought of Oscar and Evita Juarez. I had first met them when they stayed at the lodge over a couple of long weekends. Jack didn't seem to care for them, but they and I struck up a friendship that grew over time as we saw more of one another outside of the resort. I think of them as some of my closest friends.

"I called Oscar and told him what happened. Even though it was Sunday, he told me to come down to his law office right away and he would meet me there. I was so thankful to have someone who could help me figure out how to protect myself and you kids. He asked a lot of questions, then laid out a series of options I could consider, discussing the pros and cons of each one. We finally decided on offering Jack two choices, and Oscar wrote them up for me.

"After leaving Oscar's office, I returned to the resort to meet with Jack. I told him about my visit to the lawyer and the two options I had formulated. The first choice was for me to call the police immediately to report the assault. My face was swollen around the cuts, and the bruise had turned an ugly shade of purple. I would likely end up with a black eye as well. There would be no need for additional evidence. Jack would be arrested, booked, and held until they could set a bail hearing; I certainly was not going to post his bail. There would be a public record of the assault and it would no doubt be reported in the Mountain View Gazette for the whole town to see.

"The other choice was to immediately move out of the owner's suite, either into town or into the mother-in-law apartment, sign an agreement relinquishing any earned interest in the resort and its assets, immediately begin anger management therapy, and never, ever again raise his hand to me or you kids.

"I made it clear that if he failed to agree to any of those, I would press charges against him and ensure every person in

Mountain View would know what he had done. Oscar had taken pictures of the damage to my face and these photos were now in the safe at his office. I told him I would not hesitate to share them widely, now or in the future, if it came to that." Adele took a sip of her water, giving me a moment's respite from her account."

Charlie was pale and I noticed her leg was bouncing as it did when she was feeling stressed. She rose and turned to look out the window toward the lake. Adele watched her closely.

I didn't know how much more I could hear without doing… something, even though I had no idea what that would be. I let out a breath that I unconsciously been holding. I realized what a strong woman Adele was. I was so impressed that she had fought for herself and her children. I noticed that Charlie had turned back from the window and was looking directly at Adele with an expression I couldn't read. With a start, I saw that Adele had gone on as my thoughts had drifted. I refocused on her words.

"That evening, I kept you kids out of the house by taking you on a picnic at the end of the lake while your dad moved into the mother-in-law apartment. The next day, the two of us met at Oscar's office and Jack agreed, in writing, to all of the conditions without any argument."

I felt a sense of relief at Adele's last words and Charlie had lost some of the haunted look that she had worn over much of Adele's confession.

Adele continued, "Surprisingly, things were actually better after that. We were very good at running the lodge. But that's as far as it went. We never divorced. We weren't even friends. I would never forgive him."

Adele directed her next words to Charlie. "What he did to me, I now suspect he did to you as well. It makes me sick to even imagine it."

Adele took a few moments before she continued. For the first time, a few tears escaped her eyes. With a catch in her voice, she continued. "I was the adult. You were just a girl." Adele's voice cracked with emotion. "I always suspected that Jack said or did something that ruined your relationship with Jory. But despite asking both you and Jack, I never knew what it was."

"Teen years are so hard on parent-child relationships. So many things that used to be shared become secrets between peers, never parents. I always thought if he hit you or hurt you in some other way, you would come to me, but you never did. You just seemed to get sadder and sadder, until I felt I was looking at a shadow of the Charlie you used to be."

Adele picked up a Kleenex from the box beside her chair. Tears were now running freely from both of her eyes, down her cheek and onto her dress. She sobbed. "I want to...No, I need to tell you *both* how sorry I am that I didn't do things differently, and sooner. The most important job a parent has is to protect their children. I believe you needed protection from your father, and I didn't protect you. As a result, I lost my daughter for seven years and Jory lost her dearest, closest friend. Charlie, and Jory, I can't go back and do it all over again, but if there was any way, any way at all that I could, believe me I would." With her face in her hands, she said, "I will answer any questions you have and hope that you can finally trust me enough to tell me what happened between you and your dad, and between the two of you back then. Adele sat quietly waiting for Charlie's response.

I thought about the amount of damage Jack had inflicted and how the ensuing secrets magnified and prolonged the damage. I thought to myself that there would be no winners here and braced myself for what might be some harsh words from Charlie. But I had underestimated Charlie and Adele's bond and love for one another.

Charlie went to her mother, sat down on the couch next to her and took her hand. Charlie kept her hand in her mother's and began to speak. It was the sorry recitation of everything Charlie had related to me that day on the ledge. It was not any easier to hear now than it had been then.

By the time Charlie finished her story, both she and Adele were crying hot, bitter tears. In one night, they had ripped all the old scars open. It had been brutal, but I hoped it would allow them to finally begin healing. I excused myself from the room to give a little space to mother and daughter.

I went into the kitchen, poured three fingers of Maker's Mark into a tumbler, and made my way out onto the porch. As I sat on the steps, sipping the fine whiskey as I watched the moon rise over Clear Springs Lake, I thought about all the long-buried truths that had now been exposed.

An hour or so later, I heard Charlie come out onto the porch. I rose and she melted into me. We sat down together on the steps. I shared what was left of my whiskey and we both looked out over the lake. Finally, she put her arm around me and said, "I hope to God that we never have to have a conversation that painful and difficult with our children."

Adele wandered onto the porch with our sweaters on her arm. We were all exhausted after such an emotional evening. I traded my empty glass for our sweaters. Adele kissed us both goodnight and went back inside. I knew Charlie and I would talk about everything when she was ready, but not now. Hand in hand, we walked out to the Jeep.

When we arrived back at my house, I filled the bathtub with hot water and added Charlie's favorite bath salts. She loved hot baths and I thought it might be just the thing to soothe her after such an emotionally wrenching evening. I placed some candles around the tub and lit them to set a relaxing mood, then laid out fresh towels. I found Charlie in the living room staring out the window. I took her by the hand and wordlessly she followed me as I led her to the bathroom. There I helped her get undressed and into the steaming, scented water. I knew I had been right about the bath when, submerged in the fragrant water, she closed her eyes and sighed a single word: "Heavenly."

"I'll be back in a bit," I whispered, then shut the door, leaving her to soak for a bit. I returned when I judged the water would have begun to cool. I helped Charlie out of the tub, wrapped her in a fresh towel and led her to the bedroom where I shed my clothes and joined her. Our love-making that night was quiet and slow, an affirmation of our love, and a promise that our future would be so different from everything that had been laid bare this night.

CHAPTER 24

May 15, 2011

Ernie, eager for his breakfast, awakened me the next morning by patting my chin with his soft paw. It was a beautiful spring day. I slipped out of bed so as not to wake Charlie and headed for the kitchen to make breakfast. I fed Ernie, got the coffee started and thought back to Adele's revelations the night before. My thoughts were a jumbled mess that seemed to take me nowhere. I decided to concentrate on cooking the perfect omelet. Breakfast was nearly ready when I heard Charlie stirring. I called out, "Breakfast in five."

A disembodied, sleep-kissed voice called back, "Be there in four."

It felt so easy and natural to be here with Charlie. I divided the finished cheese and mushroom omelet in two, put half on each plate and added a slice of buttered toast. I'd just poured fresh coffee when Charlie joined me at the table wearing an old Henley shirt of mine and a pair of my shorts. "Good morning, Charlster. How are you feeling this morning?" I asked.

She looked up at me and smiled. "You haven't called me that in years." A look passed between us. "I've missed it."

I smiled back. "How are you feeling about the conversations with your mom last night?"

Charlie swallowed a bite of her omelet. "I feel like I ran a marathon yesterday. But I also feel...you know... oh... I'm not sure how I feel," she said with frustration. "The subject last night was awful, but today I feel... a little lighter somehow. I'm still processing everything in my head."

Still smiling, I added, "Well luckily for you, we have the whole day to ourselves and there isn't one single thing we absolutely must do. From the look of relief on Charlie's face, I knew I had set the right tone for the day. A total departure from the heaviness of the night before. Today we could just relax.

We lolled about all morning, reading the paper and online news, and checking social media to see what our friends and families were up to. Then we began talking about our summer vacation plans. We took turns sharing our ideas for what we might do or where we might go on our vacation, slowly narrowing our options down to the top four. After a lot of back and forth, we finally combined a couple of our ideas and came up with a plan. We would take a three-week camping trip in the Four Corners area of the Southwest where Utah, Arizona, Colorado, and New Mexico come together. A place where somehow you can stand in all four states at once. Neither of us had ever been there before and we both thought that there would be tons to see and do.

We decided to devote two weeks to exploring the many national parks in the Four Corners area, then use the last week to drive slowly back to Mountain View on scenic sideroads. Armed with a plan, I brought out my Atlas and some maps to begin plotting our route. A few minutes into this, I noticed that Charlie's attention had slipped away from vacation planning.

"Hey, where'd you go?" I asked.

"I was thinking about last night. I'm still trying to figure it all out. I'm so lucky that I have you to talk to. Mom really has no one. I want to check back in with her. I'd like to ask her a few more questions and I'll bet she has some more for me, too. But more importantly, we need to figure out what to do with all of it now that it's out in the open. Remember what you said about seeing a counselor to learn how to move on from the anger?"

I nodded.

"Well, I think maybe mom and I might benefit from talking with a counselor to help us find a way to leave this behind because right now, I hate that man. We need some help to move on if that's even possible. What do you think, Jory?" Charlie turned to me, wide-eyed and hopeful.

"I think that's a very good idea," I said as I put my arm around her waist.

"Would you be willing to come, too?" Charlie asked.

"Certainly."

"If Mom is available to talk some more now, would you mind if we put off our vacation planning for a bit?"

"Of course not. Could you let her know how much I respect and admire her?"

Charlie nodded and went off to find her cell phone and call her mom. She returned a few minutes later, saying she was going up to the resort.

Inspired by Charlie's wish to see her mother, I spent the rest of the morning visiting my own grandmother and mother. I found Grandma out in her garden, planting marigolds around her vegetable patch in an endless battle against the insects, rabbits and deer that found her little tract irresistible. Grandma believed in organic gardening. She used some plants to dissuade many garden pests away from other plants. Her most powerful weapon against the deer, however, was not a plant. But a motion activated sprinkler that drenched approaching deer with water before they could do any damage. A few splashes and they would hastily retreat.

Grandma went inside for a minute to get us both a glass of tea and, never one to overlook available manpower, gardening gloves for both of us. We worked companionably moving our tea glasses along the rows as we hand-weeded her garden. We caught one another up on all the important Mountain View news.

I filled her in on Charlie's job hunt, the openings at school, our upcoming vacation plans, and the class I wanted to take at the community college. In turn, she told me about Veronica White's recent fourth marriage, Renee Lucas' third child who'd been born the day before, Tawanda Rogers' promotion and the rumor that Mountain View was under consideration to be home to a new Amazon fulfillment center. I have never understood why Grandma bothered to listen to the local TV news. She was always hours, sometimes days, ahead of the media. I loved these conversations with Grandma and was very glad we lived close enough to each other to enjoy them often.

After a couple of hours, I made my goodbyes and headed over to Mom's for family visit number two. It was a gorgeous day. The sky was that bright blue that's a sure sign that summer is on its way. The azure sky and warm weather, coupled with the hundreds of variations of spring green in the trees and plants, lifted my spirits.

Mom greeted me at the door with her usual, "Hey girl!" and warm hug. We sat out on the back patio enjoying the birds and the warm day. Mom filled me in on all the happenings at the hospital. *Grey's Anatomy* had nothing on Mountain View Regional Medical Center when it came to intrigue and scandal.

Mom asked about Charlie, and I told her that she was visiting with Adele. Mom looked at me carefully. "I imagine the situation with Jack has brought some issues to the fore."

"That would be an understatement."

"How are things going?"

"Charlie and Adele are trying to work through some history that they probably should have talked about years ago. I told you what Jack said and did to Charlie. Seems like Jack engaged in similar behavior with Adele."

"You know, Adele came to see me the first night of Jack's stay at Sunrise View," my mom confided.

I remembered then, that when I took Charlie back to her cabin that night, Adele's car was not in the parking lot. At the time, I wondered where she might have gone. "I didn't know where she went that night, but I am glad it was to see you."

"Adele's life hasn't been as easy as a lot of people think. As you now know, Jack was not the man most people thought he was, either. Adele and I had dinner together that night and a long talk. I hope it helped her see a way to talking it all out with Charlie."

I looked at my mom with amazement. How did she do that? "That's exactly what happened last night. For the first time, Adele and Charlie had a long and honest conversation about Jack. It was brutal to listen to, but not as hard as living it. What he did to Adele was awful, but at least she was an adult. I think what he did to Charlie was much worse because she was so young. He created a barrier between Adele and Charlie that allowed him to get away with so many things. This morning, after thinking about it a little more, Charlie went back to talk with Adele further. It's a lot to process, but I think they're going to be okay."

My mom didn't reach out to many people, but that didn't mean she didn't care. She also knew when quiet was the best course of action. She didn't press me for more information, but she did say that she and Adele had been getting to know one another a lot better. Then she surprised me. "I could just wring that man's neck for the trouble he caused between those two good, kind women, and the pain that you suffered on account of him?"

"I'd be in line ahead of you, Mom."

"Well, we can't very well both go to jail and leave Mountain View unprotected from Grandma and Rose!" With a laugh we agreed and turned our conversation to less serious subjects.

When I arrived home in the late afternoon, I was very glad and a little surprised to see Charlie's red Miata in the driveway. As she was scheduled to substitute teach the next day, I thought that after talking some more with Adele she might have returned to her apartment rather than coming back to my house. I opened the door to find her sitting on the couch with Ernie on her lap. There was a cup of tea, and a book that she'd been reading on the end table next to her. I could hear Ernie purring from across the room.

"Hey, you. How was your visit with your mom?"

"It went really well. I'm so glad I went back today. We've decided to see a family counselor. I think that might help us all find a way to let go of some anger and hurt we still carry. It will also help mom decide how much, if anything, she should tell Theo and Raylene.

"I didn't want to go back to the apartment without seeing you and thanking you for hanging in there with Mom and me yesterday. It really was a terrible recitation: first my mom's account and then me repeating what I shared with you on the ledge. I want you to know that having you with me last night made it bearable. I know you didn't want to go through that again, but you stayed to support me. You've been my rock, Jory. I will never forget your kindness last night."

"Well, you are very welcome. I think it was a very difficult evening for all three of us. When you and I talked about it on the ledge, I was so emotional that I couldn't catch everything you said. Some things you said that day hit me so hard that my brain sort of froze. Some of the time up there, I didn't realize you were still talking because I was thinking of what you had just said. Hearing it again let me understand even more clearly what Jack did to you. I care about you so much Charlie. And I feel the same way about Adele. Hearing those things again made me love and want to protect both of you all the more."

I crossed the room and sat next to Charlie. "It's getting harder and harder to say goodbye to you at the end of the day. In fact, I think I am in danger of becoming addicted to you. Do you think the sight of the two of us arriving at MVHS on a Monday morning in the same car is going to create a scandal?"

"Well, it might be titillating for some, but it sounds kinda fun to me."

That night, lying in Charlie's arms, I felt closer to her than ever before. It was a mix of feelings: love, affection, a sense of calm, and emotional safety. I knew she would never intentionally hurt me. Despite everything Jack had made her do, she'd tried, in the best way she knew how, to protect me and her mom, too. It had caused her deep pain and sadness over many years.

I knew all parents make mistakes with their kids. But 'mistakes' are very different from the intentional acts Jack engaged in. I flashed back to Charlie's and my conversation on the porch last night. I wanted to talk to Charlie about one particular part.

I could tell by her breathing that she had not yet fallen asleep. "Charlie, when you joined me sitting out on the porch at the resort last night, I was still feeling numb from your mom's revelations. It was heartbreaking to hear again what Jack had done to you and your mother. It made me think of you and me and what our future will look like and the mistakes we'll inevitably make. When I asked you how you and your mom were doing, you said, 'I hope we *never* have to have a conversation that painful and difficult with *our* children.'"

Charlie nodded her understanding.

I scooted over, spooning even closer to her. "You said 'our children.' Charlie, do you want to have children someday?"

"I want that, Jory. Someday, I hope to have children with you."

"I want that too," I whispered."

"Kids plural?"

I thought for a moment. "There's a lot about being an only child that I really enjoyed, but when I was growing up and even now, I always thought it would have been great to have a brother or sister or both. I think having siblings helps you along in life."

"So, two kids do you think?"

"Well, two...or three."

"Well, okay then." She turned to face me. "When the time comes, I know you'll start a spreadsheet."

We looked at one another and grinned.

EPILOGUE - ONE YEAR LATER

At Charlie's words, I looked up from the Clear Springs Lake Resort photo album that I had been idly paging through.

"Yes, you *do* have to come shopping with me again," Charlie firmly stated looking directly in my eyes as if at a recalcitrant child.

I tried my best to ensure that no part of my next statement sounded whiney. "But Charlie, I picked out my dress weeks ago and you should have too. We have looked at what seems like hundreds of dresses, many of which look stunning on you. I really *don't want to* go shopping again," I whined.

When I said the word "stunning" I suddenly flashed back to our first real date almost two years ago and the oh-so-embarrassing conversation with Charlie and Adele when I stopped at the lodge to pick up Charlie. I quickly put that entire debacle out of my mind so I could continue pleading, ignoring the fact that Charlie had adopted a tone that did not bode well for my success.

"Jory, we *are* going to Boise today and we *are* going to look until we find the perfect dress. You promised all week you would come with me."

Truth reared its ugly head. I *had* promised. But when I said I'd go I didn't think I would *really* have to go. She tapped her foot and crossed her arms. Argument over. During the past year of living with Charlie I had learned to recognize when I was beat.

"Okay, okay, you're right, I did promise," I admitted. "I'll happily come along with you," I lied.

Trying to salvage what I could of the upcoming weekend, I added, "Maybe we could spend the night in Boise and see a play or go to a concert?" That would be something I could look forward to while sitting dutifully outside of the dressing rooms at the bridal stores, holding Charlie's purse, I thought to myself.

"Good idea!" Charlie agreed. "I don't know why you're dragging your feet. You know we'll have fun. We always do."

The thing is, we *did* have a good time--and the dress she found that day *was* perfect.

We were lucky enough to get tickets to *War Horse* that night, and we were excited to see the play that had received rave reviews. Adding even more to my anticipation, it was playing at the beautiful Morrison Theater, with its amazing 10-story stage and panoramic views of the city and Boise River.

After dress shopping *all day*, we had an early dinner at the Roundhouse Refectory, one of our favorite restaurants in Boise. Over dinner we talked about our wedding, our jobs at MVHS teaching English and Science respectively, Theo and Ursula's new baby boy, and our upcoming weekend with Adele, my mom, and Aunt Rose at Sun Valley Lodge. Grandma had bowed out in favor of her first poker tournament. We had high hopes for her success.

After dinner we took a ride through bustling Boise. It was growing so fast that every time we came to town there was something new to see or do. I drove us out to the airport. We parked and held hands as we watched the jets take off and land. My mind travelled back to the day I saw Charlie for the first time after seven years apart. Looking back on it, I was so grateful to my mom for thinking to ask me to go to the airport to pick up Charlie from her flight that day.

Watching a Boeing 737 jet take off, my mind wandered to our hike up the summit trail, the fall from the look-out that could have ended disastrously, Charlie's courage on the ledge when she finally shared the awful things her father had done, and Charlie's eyes when she told me that her love for me had never wavered through all our years apart. I felt my eyes fill with tears. We had come *so* close to never seeing one another again.

"Jory, what's wrong? Don't you like the dress after all?" Charlie asked anxiously.

I realized that our minds had gone in completely different directions. I felt a smile form on my face which turned into a laugh, a laugh from deep down that felt wonderful, like I might never want to stop. I truly loved this woman and her darned wedding dress, too. I knew I wanted to spend the rest of my life with her.

I suddenly couldn't wait for our wedding and future together. Times, good and bad, children, and maybe eventually, even grandchildren. She would always bring the sunshine. I would always have an umbrella. I could see it all and I knew she could too.

I reached across and drew her into a loving embrace, knowing she would understand the promise I was silently making to her. She was, forever, my Charlie.

ABOUT THE AUTHOR

Dayne Winters

I live in La Quinta California with my wife, an endlessly entertaining dog, and a cat that is the boss of us all. This is my first novel. I hope you enjoy reading this story as much as I enjoyed writing it. I would love to hear from you at daynewinters@gmail.com